THE MIGHTY

The Epic Escape From the Underworld

CRISPIN BOYER

Illustrated by Andy Elkerton

UNDER THE *Stars*

NATIONAL GEOGRAPHIC

Washington, D.C.

NATIONAL GEOGRAPHIC and Yellow Border Design are trademarks of the National Geographic Society, used under license.

Under the Stars is a trademark of National Geographic Partners, LLC.

Since 1888, the National Geographic Society has funded more than 14,000 research, conservation, education, and storytelling projects around the world. National Geographic Partners distributes a portion of the funds it receives from your purchase to National Geographic Society to support programs including the conservation of animals and their habitats. To learn more, visit natgeo.com/info.

For more information, visit nationalgeographic.com, call 1-877-873-6846, or write to the following address:

National Geographic Partners, LLC
1145 17th Street N.W.
Washington, DC 20036-4688 U.S.A.

For librarians and teachers: nationalgeographic.com/books/librarians-and-educators

More for kids from National Geographic: natgeokids.com

National Geographic Kids magazine inspires children to explore their world with fun yet educational articles on animals, science, nature, and more. Using fresh storytelling and amazing photography, *Nat Geo Kids* shows kids ages 6 to 14 the fascinating truth about the world—and why they should care. **natgeo.com/subscribe**

For rights or permissions inquiries, please contact National Geographic Books Subsidiary Rights: bookrights@natgeo.com

Designed by Amanda Larsen
Hand-lettering by Jay Roeder

Hardcover ISBN: 978-1-4263-7178-3
Reinforced library binding ISBN: 978-1-4263-7179-0

Printed in the United States of America
22/WOR/1

For Max the hilarious

—C.B.

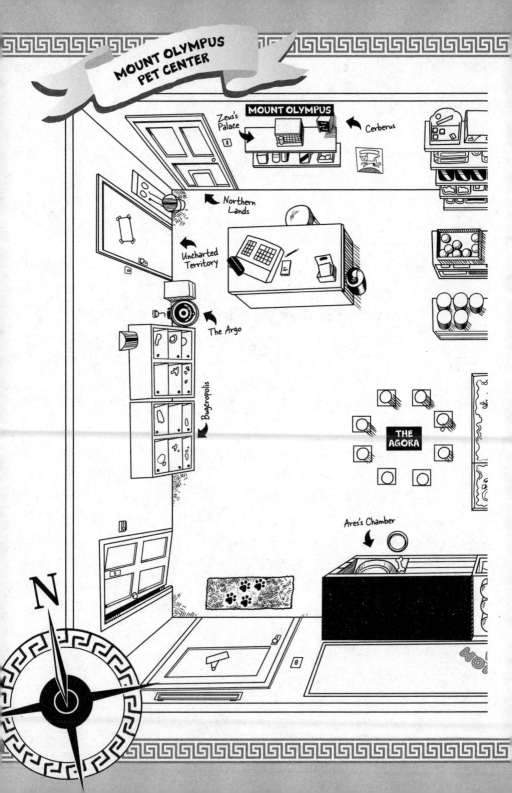

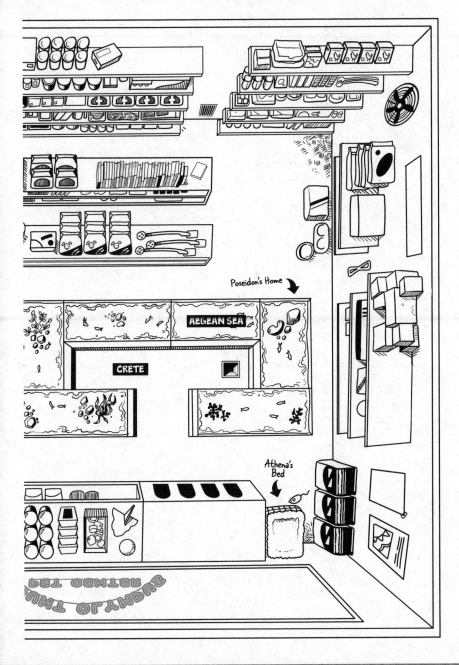

Poseidon's Home ➘

AEGEAN SEA

CRETE

Athena's Bed ➘

PET CENTER
TOWN OF ARMYS

Zeus is a golden hamster with a cloud-shaped patch on his cheek. Zeus believes he's the king of all the other animals that live at the Mount Olympus Pet Center. The favorite rescued pet of Artie, the shop's owner, Zeus genuinely cares about his fellow Olympians but also sees them as minions that should follow him on nightly adventures, which often go awry. When humans aren't around, he scrambles down from "Mount Olympus," the highest shelf in the shop where his enclosure is, and pictures himself wearing a white chiton—a fine shirt people wore in ancient Greece—and a crown-like gilded laurel wreath.

Demeter is a small grasshopper with a big heart. Once a resident of the rescue center's Bugcropolis (the city of insects), she's now Zeus's constant, loyal companion and loves to explore the shop's world. She wears a sash of lettuce over her shoulder and a laurel wreath on her head to represent the Greek goddess of the harvest, for whom she's named. The youngest and fastest of the Olympians, Demeter can fly in short bursts. But don't let her size fool you—this is one courageous grasshopper!

Athena is the wise gray tabby cat that lives under the front window of Mount Olympus Pet Center. Named after the goddess of wisdom, Athena often tries to keep Zeus out of trouble when he starts dreaming up wild adventures. Her quick and clever thinking helps settle arguments and solve problems. For instance, she figured out how to steer the *Argo*, a robot vacuum, which she now captains around the pet center. In the human world, she wears a gold collar with an owl charm, but the other Olympians see her wearing a laurel crown and two thin gold bracelets that wrap around her front paws.

Ares the pug is the strongest of the pet center Olympians. Courageous and impulsive like the god of war, Ares is the first to jump into an adventure and face any monster. But his excitement can sometimes get the better of him. (One time he accidentally sat on Poseidon's hose and almost suffocated the pufferfish!) Ares loves to be called a good boy and can eat an entire handful of Mutt Nuggets in one sitting, which probably contributes to his "meatloaf-ish" body. He wears a spiked collar and, among the Olympians, a bronze Spartan war helmet.

Poseidon is a white-spotted pufferfish that lives in the fish tank (known to the animals as the Aegean Sea) at Mount Olympus Pet Center. From his saltwater throne Poseidon rules over his fishy minions and challenges Zeus's authority over the center. The two regularly argue over who is the better ruler. Poseidon can leave his aquarium by swimming into a plastic diving helmet that has a long hose connected to the tank. He wears a tiny gold crown and carries a trident, just like the Greek god he's named after.

Hermes is the newest resident of Mount Olympus Pet Center. Rescued from a poultry ranch, she's an Appenzeller hen (or lady chicken). Ancient Greece is a new realm for Hermes, but that doesn't stop her from trying to live up to her name as the goddess of sleep. She can crow out a tune that would wake the dead! Hermes has the courage of an Amazon and helps the team soar to new heights—even if she's afraid of heights herself.

Artemis "Artie" Ambrosia is the owner of Mount Olympus Pet Center. In Greek mythology Artemis is the goddess of hunting and wild animals—so it makes sense that Artie has rescued the animals living at the center. It also makes sense that she named all her rescued animals after Greek gods, since she loves Greek mythology. She even listens to *Greeking Out*, a podcast that retells the famous myths and gives the animals crazy ideas for their adventures. Artie plans to open a rescue center next door to Mount Olympus so she can find *fur*-ever homes for more animals.

ARTEMIS AMBROSIA DIDN'T WANT TO LEAVE
Mount Olympus Pet Center, even though it was five
minutes to closing time. It wasn't only that she loved her
job as the center's caretaker, despite endless hours spent
scraping algae from the aquariums and refilling food
bowls. And it wasn't because it was storming outside—
a summer downpour just in time for her walk home.

It was that strange things happened after she left
the center each night. Chew toys went missing. Rodents
went swimming. Displays came crashing down. The shop's
robot vacuum never seemed to recharge. But that
wasn't all. A lot more happened in her pet center than
Artemis—Artie for short—could imagine.

She looked around at her favorite rescues, who she
suspected were also the most troublesome. Poseidon the
pufferfish hovered above a colorful coral in his tank.
Ares the pug nibbled on Mutt Nuggets near his kennel,
while Hermes the hen snoozed alongside him. Athena the

cat was curled up in her bed beneath the picture window and its Mount Olympus Pet Center sign. And at the back of the center, on the highest shelf, her favorite rescued animal sprinted in his exercise wheel.

"Just once I wish I could see what you mischief-makers are up to at night," Artie said.

"There's an app for that," answered a voice behind her. Artie turned to see her friend Callie in the entry to the vacant space next door, which she was converting into an expansion for the pet center.

"What kind of app?" Artie replied, intrigued. "Like a nonsense sensor?"

"More like an extra few sets of eyes," Callie said as she lugged her tool bag to the front door. "I'll show you tomorrow."

Artie had wrapped up her evening routine. She joined Callie at the door and turned off the light.

"Closing time, Zeus the Mighty," Artie called. The golden hamster looked at her. "You behave, my little escape artist. One of these nights you'll wish you never sneaked away from home!"

᙭᙭

CHAPTER 1

ZEUS THE MIGHTY WISHED HE HAD NEVER
sneaked away from home. For the first night
in as long as he could remember, his squad of
Olympian gods didn't have an adventure awaiting them:
no multiheaded monsters to vanquish, no enchanted
relics to recover, no perilous journeys to undertake.

Instead, the Olympians milled about in the Agora
while Zeus leaned against a rope-wrapped pillar,
glancing longingly at his palace. He could be on Mount
Olympus now, kicking back in his Golden Fleece bed,
popping pieces of Fuzzy Feast into his mouth.

"Watch us, Zeus! Watch! Watch!" A tan pug barreled
past the king of the Greek gods, snapping him out of his
daydream.

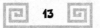

"Watch what?" Zeus straightened his royal chiton as Ares the pug continued his mad scramble. The hamster's mouth dropped when he noticed a white speckled hen perched precariously on Ares's back. "Why is Hermes riding on Ares, Demeter?" Zeus asked the grasshopper lazing nearby.

"Beats me," replied Demeter, the goddess of the harvest and Zeus's best friend. She paid little mind to the charging pug as she nibbled on the piece of lettuce draped across her shoulder.

"I believe he's trying to help Hermes fly," explained Athena the cat, who was batting at a feather hanging from the tip of a springy stick standing upright from a rubber cup stuck to the ground. Artie had given Athena the toy recently to help distract her from chasing Hermes. Athena might be the goddess of wisdom, but she was still a cat, and cats chased birds.

Zeus observed as Ares ran in a wide arc that brought him back in their direction. He now charged full speed at the assembled Olympians, his wrinkly face hidden by his Spartan war helmet. On his back, Hermes held her wings out for balance, like a surfer riding a wave.

Poseidon the pufferfish, hovering in his clear dive helmet, eyed the approaching pair with growing concern. "Should we move, perhaps?" The pug was mere feet away with no sign of slowing.

"Ares!" Zeus yelled, raising his paws and standing directly in the pug's path. "Pump the brakes!"

"Stop, stop, STOP!" Poseidon held up his trident.

But Ares wasn't stopping. Athena and Demeter leapt out of the way just as the dog was about to blast through the Olympians like a pug-shaped bowling ball. Zeus and Poseidon braced for impact.

At the last second, though, Ares dug all four paws into the ground and skidded to a halt inches from Zeus and Poseidon. Hermes kept going, catapulted off the pug's back. She pumped her wings clumsily and clawed higher and higher into the air.

It wasn't an impressive performance by most bird standards, but for a chicken, she positively soared.

"Go, go, go!" Ares encouraged, panting to catch his breath.

"Stretch your wings more!" Athena shouted, no longer interested in her toy. "You'll get more lift!"

"No, flutter your wings like this!" Poseidon yelled, wiggling his pectoral fins to demonstrate.

"I think I know more about flying than y'all!" Hermes hollered back.

The Olympians noticed that Hermes had her eyes squeezed tight against her fear of heights.

"Flying blind might not be the best idea," Ares shouted. He had pushed his Spartan war helmet back on his head so that his wrinkly pug face poked out. "Oh, watch out!"

BOOM!

Hermes had flown straight into the portal to uncharted territory. But instead of just smacking against it, she had knocked it open and continued right into the mysterious realm beyond.

"I did *not* see that coming!" Zeus said, suddenly excited.

"I don't think Hermes did, either," Demeter added.

For the first time in more than a month, the entryway to uncharted territory stood open. The land on the other side seemed dark, unlike Greece, which was lit by the Mount Olympus Pet Center sign.

But just as quickly as it had opened, the portal began to swing shut.

Zeus, keen to explore, ordered, "Olympians, prop open that portal!"

"On it!" exclaimed Athena as she leapt atop the *Argo*. The Olympians used the vessel as transportation for long trips across their realm. "Let's go, *Argo*!" She slapped a button underfoot. *BOOP!* It whirred to life and began cruising toward the portal. Zeus and Demeter hopped aboard as the *Argo* rolled past them.

"Faster, Athena! Faster!" Zeus yelled.

"Pretty sure you all know this by now, but the *Argo* only has one speed," Athena muttered as she concentrated on piloting her vessel.

Zeus figured Athena had a fifty-fifty shot at reaching the portal in time to prop it open. Good odds. He was glad he had sneaked out of Mount Olympus tonight after all.

CHAPTER 2

THENA WEDGED THE *ARGO* INTO THE
closing portal without a moment to spare.
BEEP! She shut down the motor and hopped
off the bow into uncharted territory. Demeter followed.

"Ooh, ooh! I wanna see uncharted territory!" Ares
cried. He ran toward the portal and scrambled over the
Argo after Athena and Demeter.

"Get back here, Ares!" Poseidon called. "I can't very
well surmount the *Argo* in this." He tapped the inside
of his mobile habitat with his trident. Poseidon's helmet
allowed him to travel in the realm of air-breathing
animals, but the bulky ball of plastic wasn't the most
nimble mode of transport. Poseidon moved by
swimming against the helmet's side and rolling it

forward. It received oxygen-rich water from a skinny
hose that stretched all the way to the Aegean Sea.

Ares reappeared at the portal
just as Zeus scrambled
through it. The pug ran to
the pufferfish's helmet
and grabbed it by its
lifeline, yanking it
gracelessly up and
over the *Argo* into
uncharted territory.
"Easy, you brute!"
Poseidon yelled in the
churning water as he
bounced behind Ares.

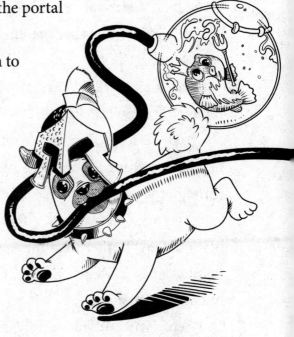

Once the water cleared and Poseidon righted himself
in his helmet, he began to take in uncharted territory,
which was cast in a dim yellow light.

It was a vast land—at least as big as their region of
Greece on the other side of the portal. And like Greece,
it was a rugged place, with towering mountains and
deep valleys. But where Greece's mountainsides were

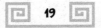

lovingly stocked by Artie with artifacts and relics, uncharted territory's were stark and empty. It was a bland land. Clearly it needed Artie's attention.

"The place smells better than I remember," Athena said, sniffing the air.

Ares took a whiff. "Yeah, not as musty. But I don't remember it looking like this."

"Y'all been here before?" asked Hermes. The speckled hen was preening her feathers after her rough flight through the portal.

"Ares and I have, once," Athena replied, "but we never got any farther than this spot." She sat down and pointed a paw at Zeus. "He's the guy to talk to about uncharted territory."

"Yep." Zeus sniffed, puffing out his chest and hiking up his chiton. "I've been all over this place. I whupped a whole colony of Harpies here, remember?"

Poseidon rolled his eyes. "And you'd still be trapped here if Athena and Ares hadn't rescued you, remember?"

"Oh, are we remembering our favorite adventures?!" Ares leapt excitedly into the center of the group. "How about when we beat the Minotaur?!"

"Before my time, buddy," Hermes chimed in. "How about when we beat the Hydra?"

"Oh, yeah!" Ares nodded, spraying slobber everywhere. "Definitely in my top ten!"

"Okay, okay, let's try to focus here." Zeus raised his paws for quiet and surveyed the landscape. "Ares made a good point. This place looks different to me, too." He started to march deeper into the gloomy landscape.

"Is this really a good idea?" Demeter peeked back the way they came. The first fingers of dawn were visible through the gap in the propped-open portal. "Artie will be back in Greece soon."

"We're here. We've got time." Zeus gestured vaguely around them. "Let's have a look-see." He marched off to the south. Athena, Ares, Hermes, and Demeter slowly followed.

But Poseidon hung back. He'd spotted a strange sea, not quite as large as the Aegean yet still impressive. East of the sea was a tall wall, beyond which buildings and other structures stretched into the gloom. He decided that if anyone lived in this walled city, they weren't there now. Even the sea looked devoid of life.

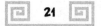

"I don't see why we should spend another moment here," Poseidon called to the others. "This place is obviously deserted."

"LEAVE HERE NOW!" boomed a deep voice.

The Olympians froze.

"This place is obviously *not* deserted," Zeus answered.

"Who said that?" Demeter asked, peering around nervously.

"Is it that Minotaur fella?" Hermes asked.

"Don't think so." Athena cocked an ear in the direction of the booming voice. "He wasn't so big on complete sentences."

"Whoever it was is in there!" Ares ran toward the eastern wall of uncharted territory. He was heading for the entrance to a massive cave barely visible in the gloom.

"Ares, no, bad god!" Poseidon shouted, but the pug ignored him. "Zeus, stop him!"

"Stop. Ares. Come back," Zeus muttered half-heartedly.

Without even slowing down, Ares disappeared into the cave.

Zeus turned to the other Olympians and shrugged. "Hey, I tried."

"You did nothing of the sort!" Poseidon fumed.

"Eh, Ares is a tough war god." Zeus waved a paw dismissively. "What's the worst that can happen?"

"Another top-ten adventure?" Hermes suggested as the group crept cautiously to the cavern's mouth.

"That's what I'm afraid of," Poseidon said.

CHAPTER 3

THE CAVE ENTRANCE WAS MORE THAN large enough for everyone to enter without ducking. Its edges were jagged, as if the opening had been chewed from the wall by a hungry beast. The Olympians could make out a green glow from deep within.

"This definitely wasn't here last time." Zeus waved at the area in front of the cave. "In fact, I remember a big vault being in the way. It's where I defeated the Harpies, you know—"

"Yes, you mentioned that already!" Poseidon snapped. "But the Harpies are gone and this cave's here now."

"And someone's living in it," Demeter added.

Athena squinted into the green gloom with her feline night vision. "Ares?" she called. "Ares! You okay in there?"

"YOUR WAR GOD IS A VERY BRAVE BOY," announced the booming voice. "I WOULD MAKE HIM MY NEW PET—IF I DIDN'T ALREADY HAVE A GUARD DOG!"

Just as the voice faded—*KRAKOW!*—thunder echoed from deep inside the cave and reverberated across uncharted territory. *KRAKOW!* The thunderclap crashed again, louder this time. A light mist issued from

within, making it impossible to see beyond the entrance.

Demeter backed up slowly. "Um, we should go."

"Not without Ares," Zeus said. He shouted into the cave: "ARES!"

"That's enough adventure for one night, buddy!" Hermes's voice was filled with concern.

The pug appeared suddenly at the cavern mouth, running so fast his helmet was barely balanced on the back of his head.

"I've never seen him so spooked," Poseidon said.

Hermes took off after her best friend, her wings pumping for a speed boost.

"I've never seen him spooked, period," said Demeter.

"It's the thunder." Athena watched Ares cower at the portal back to Greece. Hermes stood over him, unsure what to do. "He hates it. It's a dog thing."

"Well, thunder is literally a Zeus thing." Zeus stood tall and straightened his royal chiton. "I'm kinda famous for it." The king of the gods began walking toward the cave entrance. "Whatever that sound was, it wasn't thunder." He stepped through the jagged opening.

KRAKOW! The thunderclap crashed again, even louder this time.

Zeus didn't flinch. He cocked his head and listened to the thunder's echo as it faded away. "Anyone else hear that weird *gonk* sound?" he asked, his face scrunched in concentration. "I can't quite put my finger on what it—"

"TURN TAIL AND RUN LIKE YOUR GOD OF WAR!" the deep voice ordered. "THIS ISN'T YOUR REALM!"

"Of all the nerve!" Zeus crossed his arms. The cloud-shaped patch of white fur on his cheek, which twitched when he was agitated, began roiling. "You dare give orders to the king of the gods?!" He tried to shout in the same booming voice. "Who do you think you are?"

"I'M HADES," the voice boomed, "LORD OF THE UNDERWORLD."

CHAPTER 4

THE MIST THICKENED WITH EACH STEP ZEUS took, surrounding him and dampening his golden fur. It smelled of must and earth and rot.

"Zeus?" Demeter's voice came from just outside the cave. "Zeus? You there? We can't see you in this pea soup."

"Hades? The Underworld?" Zeus ignored Demeter and answered the booming voice. "Why do those names ring a bell … ?"

"The Oracle mentioned them once, in her lesson on the trials of Hairy-clees," Athena called helpfully.

"I'M THE ILL WIND THAT STEALS YOUR FINAL BREATH!" the voice boomed. "I'M THE SHADOW THAT SNATCHES DEATH FROM LIFE."

"Well, you're a real barrel of giggles." Zeus wrapped his arms across his chest as a bone-chilling breeze kicked past him, ruffling the spiky fur beneath his laurel-leaf crown. "I'm beginning to suspect we're not welcome here."

"ONLY THE DEAD ARE WELCOME IN MY REALM," continued the voice. "LEAVE NOW—UNLESS YOU WISH TO JOIN THEM."

The green glow within the cave flickered, then flared brighter. Suddenly, a large rock flew past Zeus in the mist. He was shocked to see the rock hover in midair, as if hanging from invisible strings, then soar back in his direction. He put up his paws to block it, but the rock fell at his feet.

"Did … did you guys see that?" Zeus asked the Olympians still outside the cave.

"See what?" Athena yelled, her voice faint and far away. "We can't even see you!"

"Zeus, get out of there!" Demeter cried.

"LISTEN TO YOUR LITTLE FRIENDS," boomed Hades. "THIS IS YOUR LAST CHANCE!"

As Hades's voice faded, the rock at Zeus's feet flew into the air again and hovered inches from his face. It drifted closer, threatening to bop him right on his crown. He began retreating slowly, but the rock stayed with him. Finally, as Zeus stumbled back into uncharted territory, it fell to the ground, its invisible strings cut.

KRAKOW!! This thunderclap was the loudest yet.

"Yipppp!" Ares scrambled over the *Argo* and back through the portal. But his frightened escape dislodged the vessel. It rolled slowly backward, pushed by the weight of the portal, which was sliding shut.

Hermes grabbed the portal with both wings and yanked, trying to keep it from closing. It was no use.

"We're about to become permanent residents!" she cried, her feet scraping against the ground.

"Everyone back through the portal!" Athena commanded.

"Don't have to tell me twice!" Demeter shouted. She reached the portal and leapt through in just three strides of her powerful grasshopper legs. She was followed by Hermes and Athena, who wedged her fluffy gray body into the narrowing gap.

"Hurry up, you two," Athena called back to Poseidon and Zeus as she strained to keep the portal open. "I can't hold this forever!"

"Just long enough for me will do." Poseidon rolled his dive helmet under Athena.

Zeus took one last look at the cave entrance. "This isn't over between us, Hades!" he yelled.

KRAKOW!! Zeus darted past Athena. She backed into Greece and let the portal close with a loud click.

The Olympians were home. Zeus eyed his realm, which was now lit by dawn, and couldn't believe what he saw. Greece was a mess. It looked as if it had been struck by an earthquake.

"What in blazes happened here?" Zeus asked as he surveyed the wrecked landscape.

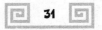

CHAPTER 5

"**A**RES HAPPENED HERE." DEMETER pointed toward the pug, who was still shaking inside his chambers far to the south. Hermes stood over him, trying her best to comfort the cowering god of war.

"That last thunderclap really threw him over the edge," the hen explained. She patted Ares awkwardly with a wing. "He tore through Greece like the Hydra."

"The Hydra never made a mess like this." Athena pawed at her stick toy, which had toppled to the ground. Crates and relics that Artie had carefully stacked on the mountainsides were scattered and smashed.

"Well, I'll be going home now," Poseidon said curtly after a brief look at the wreckage. He rolled hurriedly to

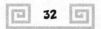

the edge of the Aegean Sea and waited as his seahorse minions began hauling him home by his lifeline. He turned inside his helmet to address the Olympians. "Good luck with … this." He waved vaguely at the debris.

Zeus, Demeter, and Athena exchanged panicked looks. They would never be able to undo Ares's damage—even if they teamed up and used all their Olympian mojo. So with Artie bound to return at any moment, they scattered.

Zeus and Demeter made it back to their palace on Mount Olympus just in time to see Artie enter the main portal of Greece, keys in hand. She was followed by Callie, and Zeus wondered if the jagged entrance to the Underworld was her handiwork.

"Good morning, Olympians," Artie said, stashing her keys in her pocket. "Everyone ready for breakfa— Oh, you've got to be kidding!" Greece's disastrous state had stopped her dead in her tracks.

Callie stepped up behind her and surveyed the tumbled boxes and knocked-over displays. "Well, *someone* had a busy night." She dropped her heavy green tool bag at her feet.

Without another word, Artie began collecting the scattered boxes of treats, ball chuckers, and pet-care books. Callie watched her for a moment, then joined in. Soon, both women had Greece organized.

"Artie took that a lot better than I expected," said Demeter, watching the cleanup effort from the pillars of the palace while nibbling from her lettuce sash.

"Whatever," Zeus said. He was already curled up on his piece of Golden Fleece, nursing his pride after his humiliating send-off from Hades in the Underworld. "She can't blame this mess on us."

Below them, Artie settled on the stool behind the cash register. "Last night you said you had something to help me keep an eye on these monsters," she said to Callie. "Lay it on me."

"Not a moment too soon." Callie rummaged through her green bag and pulled out a colorful box. "Voilà."

"What's Callie got?" Demeter asked. When Zeus didn't answer, Demeter turned and found him already fast asleep, his crown pulled over his eyes.

"If you don't care, I don't care," Demeter muttered. She hopped to her bed nook at the back of the palace

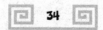

and shut her eyes for a nap.

Zeus felt like he had barely slept a wink when he was jolted awake by a strange feeling—like he was being watched. He rubbed the sleep from his eyes. That's when he saw the source of his unease.

A four-sided structure he had never seen before loomed just outside his palace on the rocky summit of Mount Olympus. It was about a quarter of the size of Zeus's palace, with smooth gray walls. As Zeus watched, the structure rotated silently on its base, revealing a dark portal on one of its four sides. Zeus couldn't see into the opening—the interior was lost in darkness—but he could sense a presence inside. The structure wasn't vacant.

Zeus sat bolt upright and squeaked in alarm.

As if in response, a pair of fearsome red eyes appeared in the portal and locked on to Zeus. From the structure's dark depths came a piercing howl— "AH-WOOOOOOOO!"

CHAPTER 6

EUS SAT FROZEN AS THE LAST ECHOES OF
the howling faded. He returned the object's
angry red stare. Suddenly, two more pairs of
eyes—one a bright white—emerged within the dark
portal. Zeus rolled off his Golden Fleece and crouched
behind it out of sight of the watchful eyes.

"Wha-what's that racket?" Demeter muttered sleepily
from her bunk at the back of the palace.

"Shush!" Zeus shot back. He peeked his head above
the Fleece just high enough to glimpse the structure.
The eyes had disappeared, and the portal was once again
dark. Then the whole structure rotated away from Zeus
to look out over Greece. "Demeter!" Zeus snapped.
"We're not alone!"

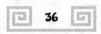

The urgency in Zeus's voice alarmed Demeter more than his actual words. She hopped atop the Golden Fleece, then nearly fell over when she saw the new gray structure just outside. "Where'd that thing come from?!"

"Take cover before it sees you!" Zeus hissed.

The grasshopper held her ground atop the Fleece. "Before what sees me?"

As if to answer Demeter, the structure—and its portal—spun back in their direction. Zeus crouched behind the Fleece, waiting for the angry howl when whatever lived inside saw Demeter. But he heard nothing.

"Hello?" Demeter shouted at the dark portal that now faced her. "Anybody in there?"

"Don't taunt it, Demeter!" Zeus stood up in full view of the portal.

"AH-WOOOOOOOO!" The red flashing eyes locked on to Zeus first, joined a moment later by the bright white eyes.

"Gah!" Zeus dropped out of sight again. The howling ceased, and the eyes faded to blackness. The structure resumed its rotation, panning out over Greece, as if keeping vigil.

Demeter, meanwhile, had remained in plain sight of those angry eyes the whole time, yet they seemed to have looked right through her. "Whoever lives in that thing, Zeus," she said in a low voice, "they don't seem to care about me."

Zeus peeked up from his hiding spot. "Oh, so suddenly, you're the expert on … whatever that is?"

Demeter hopped off the bed and strolled casually to the palace pillars closest to the structure as it rotated slowly back in her direction. She waved four legs, trying to rouse whatever was within, but the portal remained dark and empty as it rotated away from her. She smirked back at Zeus and poked a leg at her chest. "Expert!"

"What's with all the howling?" Artie exclaimed. She had been arranging a display of tomes about cats.

"That's Cerberus!" Callie cried excitedly. "Good Cerberus! Good dog!"

"Sir-bur-us?" Demeter repeated the name slowly as she peered into the portal rotating in her direction.

"I remember that name—the Oracle said Cerberus is the guard dog of the Underworld!"

"Hold up! Do you mean Hades's mutt is in that doghouse?!" Zeus hissed from his hiding spot.

"Cerberus? I love the name," Artie told Callie. "Although that howl is a bit much."

"I'm sure we can pick a different sound." Callie reached up and grabbed the structure, then turned it over in her hands. "Let's see what Cerberus saw. Hmmm, the flashing red lights are the motion sensor, so Cerberus definitely detected something moving. It can notice anything Zeus-size or larger, and I adjusted it to ignore anything human size. It's no use if we set the dog off. The bright white lights are for the camera. And then it has a special sensor with purple lights that helps the whole system see at night. Artie, check your phone—it should have uploaded the video it just took."

"What, really?" Artie reached into her back pocket and pulled out the black rectangular device she carried with her everywhere. Her fingers raced over its glassy surface. Callie looked over her shoulder. "All right, here's the video," Artie said.

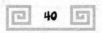

"Huh," Callie said, scrutinizing the screen, "looks like it recorded Zeus's empty little bed." She looked up from the device into Zeus's palace. Callie wasn't nearly as tall as Artie, so she had to crane her neck and stand on her tippy-toes.

"Quick, hide!" Zeus cried to Demeter. The grasshopper leapt behind the Fleece.

"What are you doing skulking around back there?" Artie asked, pointing at Zeus.

"He must've triggered Cerberus's motion sensor," Callie explained. "But maybe the noise scared him off his bed before the day camera could capture him." She fiddled with something on the hound's back. "The system just needs some fine-tuning. I'll set Cerberus so he's not so sensitive."

"Yeah, I don't really need him howling every time Zeus rolls out of bed." Artie walked back to the display she had been organizing, then stopped and turned back. "Speaking of howling, any way to change that alarm to something less ... I don't know, terrifying?"

"Sure," Callie said, still fiddling with the hound's back. "Just a few tweaks and Cerberus here will be ready

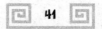

for duty, all the time, day or night. You'll never be surprised by your critters' midnight antics again."

Callie set Cerberus back in its spot. She noticed Zeus watching her nervously. "You hear that, little guy?" she said. "With Cerberus on the lookout, you'll never set paw outside your habitat without us knowing. You're going *nowhere.*"

Zeus watched the doghouse resume its slow back-and-forth rotation. A sense of dread filled his belly.

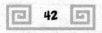

CHAPTER 7

EMETER CREPT TO ZEUS'S SIDE. "YOU OKAY, pal?" she asked the hamster.

"Fabulous. Never better. Tip-top," Zeus snapped. He'd crossed his arms. The white patch of fur on his cheek began twitching.

"Really? You don't seem tip-top," Demeter replied.

Zeus exploded. "HE'S GOT A LOT OF NERVE!"

"He *who*?" Demeter looked confused. "Hades or Cerberus?"

"BOTH!" Zeus raged. "Let's start with Hades: He had the gall to order me out of his dumb cave! ME! Can you believe it?"

"Unbelievable." Demeter shook her head, then repeated, "Unbelievable."

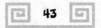

"It's bad enough that Poseidon thinks he reigns over any puddle or drop of water. Now I got this new guy claiming the entire Underworld!"

"You're still Zeus the Mighty, king of the gods," Demeter said, trying to rally his spirits. "You evicted the Harpies! You vanquished the Minotaur! You toppled the Hydra! You'll figure this out!"

Zeus threw up his paws. "And now I've got Hades's three-headed hound watching me around the clock!" He waved helplessly toward Cerberus in his house outside the palace. "As if being king of the gods wasn't already stressful enough. Planning our nightly adventures, protecting the realm—that's going to be a little trickier if I can't actually leave Mount Olympus." He slumped to the floor. "Hades has beaten me. He wins. And I haven't even met the guy face to face!"

Demeter struggled for something reassuring to say. When familiar harp music suddenly filled the air, she sighed with relief. "The Oracle's about to give us a lesson! She'll know what to do!"

Zeus's ears perked up. Staying low to avoid the hound's sweeping gaze, he crept to the pillars along the southern edge of the palace with Demeter. Below, he saw Artie fiddling with her rectangular device, and the harp music grew louder before fading as a voice began speaking: "Welcome to Greeking Out, your weekly podcast that delivers the goods on Greek gods and epic tales of triumphant heroes. I'm your host, the Oracle of Wi-Fi."

Zeus glanced over at the doghouse, curious if Cerberus was distracted by the Oracle's lesson. No flashing eyes appeared at the dark portal, but it was still sweeping left and right. Clearly, this guard dog didn't care about the Oracle's endless wisdom and fortunes foretold.

"Today," the Oracle continued, "we'll embark on a journey to one of the most frightening realms in Greek mythology: the Underworld."

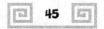

Zeus and Demeter exchanged knowing glances. This was a lesson they did not want to miss.

"Our tale explores a vast land never touched by the sun," the Oracle explained. "A kingdom of the dead and a prison for the castoffs of the sunlit lands—all ruled by a cunning god."

"Hades." Demeter spit out the name.

"This episode of *Greeking Out* is brought to you by Extra Pounce Cat Toys," the Oracle continued. "Keep your feline feelin' fine with Extra Pounce."

"Get on with it!" Zeus shouted.

The Oracle did: "The Underworld is a land cast in permanent shadow, every corner steeped in mystery. Even its landmarks and regions have ominous names, such as the Fields of Mourning or Tartarus, a prison that not even a god could escape. And while the Underworld might sound like a frightening place to visit, it possesses a unique beauty that rivals the scenic wonders of Greece."

"That dank dump rivals *my* realm?" Zeus groused. "Gimme a break."

"The sky glitters with a magical light, casting a strange glow over mountain ranges, otherworldly forests, bottomless lakes, dark marshes, and five rivers of enchanted water. Each river is tied to a different emotion or ill effect. Anyone who drinks from the muddy currents of the River Lethe falls into a trancelike state. The black waters from the River Acheron produce an intense sense of misery. The Underworld's entrance is marked by the River Styx, raging in both its swirling current and the emotions it produces. Only the boatman Charon can ferry visitors across it."

"Kah-run?" Demeter pronounced the name carefully. "Hades has his own boatman?"

"Who cares about some leaky ol' rowboat?" Zeus retorted. "We got Athena and the *Argo*."

"Once across the Styx, visitors become permanent residents. Their lives in the surface realm cease." Demeter sat rapt. Zeus yawned.

"Strange and powerful creatures lurk in this dim land," the Oracle continued, "yet none stranger or more powerful than the Underworld's king, the mysterious god Hades. Just as Zeus commands all in the sunlit realm and Poseidon rules the seas, Hades reigns in the Underworld, feared and respected by all his subjects."

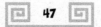

"I am so over hearing how great this Hades guy is."
Zeus turned away and began inspecting his paws.

"And just as Poseidon wields his trident and Zeus has his thunderbolts," the Oracle explained, "Hades possesses his own powerful artifact: the Cap of Shadows. Its magical energies trick the eyes of mortals and immortals alike. When Hades slips it on, he becomes invisible."

"Invisible!" Demeter glanced toward Cerberus's house. "A cap like that sure would come in handy."

"Handy for what? Cheesy magic tricks?" Zeus retorted.

CHAPTER 8

"The Cap of Shadows is Hades's most precious treasure," the Oracle said. "He hides it deep within the Underworld, in the throne room of his mazelike estate. The House of Hades sits on the banks of the River Acheron, and those nimble, cunning, resilient, and strong enough to reach it must contend with the most fearsome sentry of all: Hades's pet, the three-headed watchdog Cerberus."

"Cerberus!" Demeter echoed.

"Yep." Zeus glanced up from his paws. "That's his name."

"And that concludes this episode of *Greeking Out*," the Oracle said. "Tune in next time to hear ..."

"What a waste of time." Zeus threw up his paws and

headed toward his bowl of Fuzzy Feast at the back of his palace. "The Oracle was no help at all."

"What do you mean, no help at all?" Demeter replied. "She gave us the key to everything!"

"Key? What key? I stopped listening the tenth time she said how great Hades is."

"The Cap of Shadows! Hades's magical invisibility hat!" Demeter said. "If you had that, you could come and go from Mount Olympus whenever you wanted, day or night!"

Zeus perked up. "True, Cerberus can't guard what he can't see. But how could we get our hands on that cap? Didn't the Oracle say it's somewhere deep in the Underworld?"

"Exactly!" Demeter said enthusiastically. "And she told us right where to find it!"

"She did?"

"Hades's throne room!"

"Oh, right, sure … Hades's throne room," Zeus repeated.

"And not only do we know where it is," Demeter carried on, "we know who's not guarding it. Him!"

Demeter jabbed a leg toward Cerberus's rotating doghouse. "Hades sent his best watchdog to keep an eye on you instead of his treasure!"

Zeus broke into a sly grin. "Demeter, are you suggesting we should heist Hades's Cap of Shadows?"

Demeter winced. "I don't know if 'heist' is the right word. Since when do we Olympians steal?"

"Oh, come on!" Zeus huffed. "Hades played dirty first. He needs to learn a lesson. It's only fair."

Demeter shrugged. "I'd feel a lot better if we were just borrowing the Cap for a while and not stealing it."

"Oh, sure, of course, we're just 'borrowing' the Cap," Zeus reassured her. But then his face fell. "Wait, how can I lead the Olympians on a heist with Six-Eyes over there watching me?"

"Well, that's the thing," Demeter replied. "You can't."

"I can't?"

"But I can."

"You?"

"Yes, me! I mean, I'm already invisible to Cerberus—Callie said it doesn't care about anything smaller than you—so I can go round up the Olympians."

"No offense, buddy," Zeus said gently, "but leading that squad of gods is a lot more work than just tying a sprig of lettuce around your neck and … uh, whatever else you do."

"I'm the goddess of the harvest," Demeter replied flatly.

"Look," Zeus continued, "I know I make this look easy and all, but I'm me and … you're … well …"

Demeter crossed four legs across her chest. "I'm what?"

Zeus glanced across Greece and saw Artie and Callie getting ready to leave for the night. Then Cerberus's portal swept in his direction.

"You're my only shot at getting back at that Hades creep," he finally said, turning back to Demeter.

"Gee, thanks for the pep talk." Demeter crept to the pillars of the palace. "I can do this, Zeus. I'll take the crew, and we'll borrow the Cap for you. In the meantime, enjoy your night off."

"Doing what?" Zeus looked around helplessly.

"I dunno." Demeter waved around the palace. "Put your feet up on the Fleece. Work on your action figures.

Make nice with your new pet over there." She jabbed a leg at Cerberus.

Zeus scowled. Down in Greece, Artie met Callie at the main portal.

"This night'll be the first test of Cerberus," Callie said. "If any of your crazy critters step foot out of their habitats, they'll get caught on camera."

"I'd say stay out of trouble, Olympians," Artie said, "but I want to see what you're all up to." She switched off the light and stepped out the door. "Nighty night."

Callie was on her heels. "In other words, go nuts!" she added as she let the portal close behind her.

Zeus waited for them to leave, then turned to Demeter. "How are you going to assemble the Olympians if they're all trapped in their chambers by the mutt hut here?"

Demeter frowned at Zeus. "Obviously I need a diversion."

Zeus looked at Cerberus and tapped his fingers together. "Okay, I'll buy you some time." He hopped over his Golden Fleece and charged toward the edge of his palace facing Cerberus. "Here, poochy, poochy, poochy!"

he yelled as he stuck his arms between the pillars and waved wildly.

Immediately, flashing red eyes appeared. "Woof! Woof! Woof!" the beast within barked in alarm, alerting the other two heads. Bright white eyes lit up, and the third head's eyes flashed a deep purple. "That's right," Zeus yelled. "Keep all your eyes on me! For I am Zeus the Mighty, king of the gods!"

"Woof! Woof! Woof!" the first head barked in reply.

Zeus turned back toward Demeter. "What are you waiting for? Go!"

Satisfied that all three of Cerberus's heads would remain focused on Zeus and not notice anyone else, Demeter squeezed through the pillars at the front of the palace, unfolded her wings, and leapt into the night.

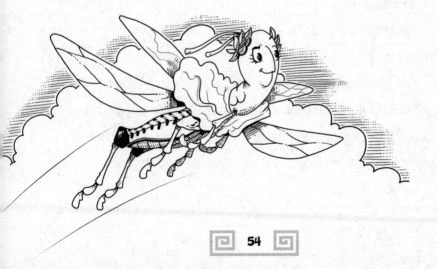

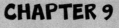

CHAPTER 9

DEMETER HIT THE GROUND RUNNING. THE clock was ticking. She needed to lead the Olympians to uncharted territory while Zeus held Cerberus's attention. She was thrilled by the prospect of taking charge. If only her old friends in the Bugcropolis could see her now.

Maybe they could! Demeter glanced toward the walled city of the insects to the west and could just make out a few dozen pairs of eyes below twitching antennae. The leggy residents were indeed watching her from the walls. Demeter gulped.

"Olympians, assemble!" she tried to shout, but her voice squeaked on the second word. She took a moment to clear her throat and tried not to think about everyone

in the Bugcropolis staring at her. "Olympians,
ASSEMBLE!"

Her voice echoed across Greece as loudly as Zeus's.
Even the king of the gods on Mount Olympus heard it.
But when he paused his waving to try to find Demeter,
Cerberus lost interest in him and began to rotate back
toward Greece. Zeus panicked.

"Me! Me! Look at me, poochy!" he exclaimed,
reaching his arms through the pillars and waving
frantically at the hound.

"Woof! Woof! Woof!" the closest head
barked in alarm as its eyes flashed red. The eyes
of the other two heads also focused on Zeus.

Down on the plains of Greece, the Olympians stood on the shore of the Aegean Sea, watching as Poseidon slowly dropped to the ground in his dive helmet.

"How come Zeus gets to play with the new doggy but I can't?" Ares whined.

"Oh, that doggy is not a good boy," Athena explained. "Probably the worst boy, in fact."

Ares growled up at Mount Olympus.

Once Poseidon had touched down on land, he glanced around at the assembled Olympians, then up at Mount Olympus. "I see our king is in for the evening."

"He'll be in for every evening with that Cerberus hound watching over him," Athena said.

"Not if my plan works!" Demeter responded.

"Your plan?" Ares cocked his head. "Is Zeus letting you run the show tonight?"

"Not like he has a choice." She jabbed a leg toward Cerberus and Zeus.

"Right," Athena realized. "You're the only Olympian small enough to evade the hound's senses."

"What are ya cookin' up?" Hermes asked.

"A heist!" Demeter announced.

"A heist?!" Ares repeated excitedly. He raced off along the shore. "A heist! A heist! We're doing a heist!" He spun around and darted back to Demeter, panting hard. "What's a heist?"

"It's a crime," Athena said skeptically. "Since when is crime our thing?"

"Okay, okay," Demeter said, waving her legs, "maybe 'heist' isn't quite the right word. We're not stealing anything—we need to borrow Hades's Cap of Shadows."

"It's a borrowing! It's a borrowing!" Ares repeated as he raced along the shore again.

"The Cap that Oracle lady was talkin' about?" Hermes asked. "Why?"

"So our king can give Cerberus up there the slip," Athena said. "Right, Demeter?"

"Exactly!" Demeter replied. "Well, that and Zeus wants to show Hades who's boss, but mostly the first thing."

"It is the sensible thing to do," Athena admitted. "Our team will never be whole with Cerberus on duty. He's bad for our mojo. If we can get Zeus that cap, he'll figure out how to defeat that watchdog permanently."

"Let's get to uncharted territory," Demeter said. "Zeus can't hold that hound's attention all night."

Ares stopped spinning and stared at Demeter, his ears and tail drooping. "Uncharted territory?" he repeated. "The place with all the scary banging and thunderclapping?"

"We can't nab the Cap from the lord of the Underworld without actually going into the Underworld, so …" Demeter shrugged.

"Nope." Ares sunk to the floor and pulled his Spartan war helmet over his head. "Nope, nope, nope."

"Well, if Ares isn't going, why should I?" Poseidon asked. "That watchdog seems to care little for my realm."

"Poseidon," Athena said, "you do realize we're only out here in the open because Zeus is up there distracting that beast?"

Poseidon reluctantly nodded.

"We all have a stake in this," Demeter said. "This heist—er, borrowing—will take a team effort."

"Nuh-uh, count me out," Ares said. "I wouldn't go back in there for all the Mutt Nuggets in the world." He squished himself flat and tried to crawl into his helmet.

CHAPTER 10

ERMES WAVED THE OTHER OLYMPIANS
away. "I GOT THIS," she mouthed to them
as she stepped up to Ares and rapped on his
helmet. "You got room for me in there, buddy?"

"Sure," replied the war god, his voice muffled as
he scooched deeper into his helmet. "You scared of the
thunder, too?"

"Me? Naw." Hermes patted the pug's tan back
soothingly. "But that's only because I got my thunder-
repellin' chain."

Ares slid his wrinkly head out of his helmet.
"Thunder-repelling chain?"

"Yep," Hermes said, puffing out her chest to display
the silver chain that ran across it. "The chain I got from

Hippolyta, queen of the Amazons, remember? It blocks thunder, fireworks, the sound of loud chewing—really, any nasty noise."

Ares cocked his head and stared at Hermes's chain. "Really? Gosh, I wish I had one of them."

Hermes scratched her red, beardlike wattles slowly. "I reckon I'd be willing to let you borrow it for this, er, borrowing thing we're doing."

"Really?!" Ares leapt to his feet, his tail a blur.

"You're the only Olympian I'd trust it with." Hermes pulled the chain over her wing, then strung it carefully through Ares's collar. "Least I could do for my best pal."

Ares's face scrunched up even more than usual as he gazed at his powerful new artifact. "Oh, I am so ready for the Underworld now!" He slipped his head into his Spartan war helmet in one smooth motion. "Hop aboard, buddy! We have a cap to borrow!"

Hermes leapt onto Ares's back with a flourish of her wings. The pug took off at a run, darting past the Olympians. "Prepare for takeoff!" he barked to Hermes. "Just like last time."

Hermes fluffed her feathers. "All systems go!"

Right when it seemed like Ares would smack straight into the portal, he dug all four paws into the ground and skidded to a halt. Hermes once again catapulted off the pug's back and pumped her wings to gain a meager altitude. And just like last time, she forced open the portal to uncharted territory with a click and sailed through to the other side.

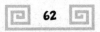

"Olympians, through the breach before it closes!" Demeter commanded. Athena, Poseidon, and Ares didn't hesitate.

"We're ... we're not gonna make it!" Ares panted.

As the portal was swinging shut, a white speckled wing appeared in the gap, followed by Hermes's head. Her crest of stubby feathers wobbled in all directions. "Hurry!" she hollered.

Athena leapt over her, while Demeter and Poseidon passed beneath her straining wings. But as Ares approached, Hermes's eyes went wide. "Whoa, whoa, buddy, slow down!"

He knocked them both into uncharted territory, and the portal fell shut with a click.

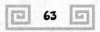

CHAPTER 11

 N MOUNT OLYMPUS, ZEUS'S ARMS FELT
like cooked spaghetti noodles and his voice
was becoming hoarse. "Show's over, mutt," he
said to the three-headed hound, which still had all three
pairs of eyes focused on him. Zeus pulled his arms back
inside the palace and stepped away from Cerberus. The
hound's eyes went dark. Its guard house swiveled away,
scanning Greece.

Zeus slurped from his water bottle, then stumbled
to the front of his palace. He saw no sign of his fellow
gods. "Some watchdog you are, pooch," he muttered,
not expecting the hound to answer. "You just let five
Olympians hit the road right under your nose." Then
he noticed the portal to uncharted territory was closed.

"Huh. Well, this definitely complicates things."

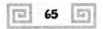

Meanwhile, the Olympians gathered around Athena while she examined the closed portal in the dim light. She pushed on it with a paw, but it didn't budge. They knew the portal opened just one way—toward them—and right now it was shut tight.

"How come everyone's so tense?" asked Ares. He was excitedly spinning in circles trying to admire his new chain.

"It probably has something to do with us all being trapped in uncharted territory," Poseidon replied.

Ares looked up in surprise. "Trapped? Here? How did that happen?"

Athena stared daggers at Ares. "Gosh, I have absolutely no idea."

Demeter stepped into the middle of the group. "We can worry about getting home later. The important thing is we made it here without Cerberus noticing. Let's go get what we came for."

"The black hat!" Ares barked excitedly.

"The Cap of Shadows," Athena corrected.

"We got nothin' better to do," Hermes agreed. "I bet we could find something down in the Underworld that will help us get home."

"Ooh, yeah!" Ares leapt to his feet. "I'll go!" He bolted toward the entrance to Hades's realm.

"Ares, get back here!" Demeter commanded. "You don't even know what you're looking for!"

The pug ignored her, so Demeter tried a different tact. "Don't forget the thunder!"

But Ares didn't slow a beat.

"What's gotten into him?" Poseidon asked.

Hermes chuckled. "I let him borrow my thunder-repellin' chain," she said.

"Thunder-repelling chain?" Demeter looked confused. "What's that?"

"I'm assuming Hermes lent him Hippolyta's belt and made up some enchantments to go along with it to bolster our war god's confidence," Athena said, nodding at Hermes. "But Ares blundering into the Underworld won't exactly help us borrow Hades's cap. Demeter, I think you should head off our thick-skulled friend."

"On it!" Demeter, fastest of the Olympians, leapt ahead of the pug in just three jumps. "Ares, Ares, stop!" She raised four legs and closed her eyes.

Ares skidded to a halt and began chewing on a foot. "So what's the plan, grasshopper?" he asked. The other Olympians caught up and watched Demeter expectantly.

Demeter opened her mouth, then clapped it shut. Her throat suddenly felt dry. She squirmed a little under everyone's gaze. "Zeus was right," she whispered. "He *does* make this look easy."

"What's that?" Athena asked, pointing her fluffy gray ears toward Demeter. "Speak up."

Demeter took a breath and composed herself. "The Oracle said the Cap of Shadows is in the throne room of

the House of Hades, where it's normally under constant guard by Cerberus." She let the other Olympians soak up the significance of her words.

Athena got it first. "But he's busy guarding Zeus. That means the Cap should be easy pickings!"

"Exactly." Demeter clapped two legs together. "Now the Oracle said only the most nimble, cunning, resilient, and strong could reach Hades's inner sanctum." She observed the Olympians gathered around her. "That describes all of us, together. So I was thinking we could split up the leadership duties, like maybe vote for whoever is best for the situation at hand."

"You're describing a democracy," Athena said. She looked toward the cave and flexed a paw. "Well, I'm the most nimble. How about I take the lead first?"

Demeter broke into a broad smile. "All in favor, say 'aye.'" She, Hermes, and Poseidon repeated, "Aye."

"I what?" Ares looked mystified.

"Are you cool with Athena leading?" Hermes asked.

"Sure!" Ares barked.

Athena began slinking to the cavern entrance. "Olympians, it's time to get stealthy."

CHAPTER 12

THE ANIMALS CREPT AS QUIETLY AS THEY could. "Watch how I walk," Athena whispered to the Olympians. "Try using just the pads of your feet." The gray cat moved like a ghost.

"Easy for you to say," Poseidon grumbled as he rolled his helmet along, trying to keep it from thumping on the floor.

Hermes made her best effort to avoid tapping her claws on the ground. Demeter couldn't make a sound if she tried. But Ares bumbled along, panting noisily, Hermes's chain jangling against his collar, his paws pounding with each step.

"Do you even know what stealthy means?" Demeter whispered to him.

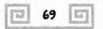

"Aye!" Ares shouted.

"SHHHH!" the Olympians all hissed.

This time when they arrived at the cave entrance, no booming voice greeted them. No smelly fog issued forth. The green glow was still visible, however.

"Hey, no thunder!" Ares exclaimed.

The other Olympians cringed, expecting the sound-and-light show from before. Instead, it remained quiet. Athena peered into the cave depths with her keen night vision, then turned and gave a shrug.

"Maybe nobody's home?" Hermes said hopefully.

"That seems unlikely," Poseidon replied. "I suppose Athena's stealthy approach is working." He saluted the cat.

Athena nodded, the owl charm she wore around her neck glinting faintly, and padded into the darkness. From what she could see, the cavern appeared to be carved from stone and clay. Tree roots and iron pipes snaked along the walls. Rocks protruded in places. She ducked beneath what she assumed was a root, but upon closer inspection looked more like a bone. "Gah!"

"What's wrong?" Demeter asked from behind her.

"Nothing, nothing," Athena said. "Just stepped on a pebble." She didn't want to alarm the other Olympians—or point out a bone to Ares, who could never resist gnawing on them.

Soon the walls closed in, narrowing to a tunnel barely large enough to fit Athena. "Bit of a squeeze here," she called over her shoulder. The Olympians had formed a single-file line behind her.

"This place reminds me of the Minotaur's maze," Poseidon said once his eyes had adjusted to the dim light, "except with a green glow instead of an orange one."

"It's mustier," said Demeter. The air around them felt wet, and it was hard to breathe.

"And cooler," Ares said, shivering slightly, so that his chain rattled against his collar.

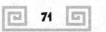

"Hush," whispered Athena. "Something's ahead."

The light in front of them flared brighter, framed by what appeared to be the tunnel's exit. They could also detect a gurgling noise, barely audible.

"What's that sound?" Demeter asked.

"Rushing water," Poseidon replied.

"You sure?" Hermes had cocked her head to listen.

"Who do you think you're talking to?" Poseidon swooshed his fins in his water-filled habitat.

Athena stepped through, and the glow grew so bright it dazzled her eyes for a moment. When she recovered, her mouth dropped open. She couldn't believe what she was seeing.

CHAPTER 13

AS THE OTHER OLYMPIANS SPILLED OUT of the tunnel, they each shielded their eyes against the light. When their vision adjusted after a few seconds, they stood gobsmacked at the fantastic vista before them.

It sprawled as far as they could see, a realm of rocky hills, dim valleys, mushroom meadows, and lakes that glittered. They were still underground—the ceiling of this realm arched high above them and was covered with a moss that shone like green fire, the source of the subterranean glow. A mazelike network of long metal tubes crisscrossed the moss on the ceiling of the cavern.

Ares's helmet wobbled as he tried to look everywhere at once. "This cave, it's so ... so cavernous."

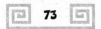

"So this is the Underworld," Athena added, her blue eyes wide. "I bet those tubes up there are the Minotaur's maze—except now we're seeing them from below."

"I do believe you're right," Poseidon said, straining to see the cavern's boundaries. "This place does seem as large as Greece."

"Wonder what they got to eat!" Ares was already bored by the fantastic terrain.

Next to them, a river flowed from a crack in the cavern wall and coursed across their path. It was filled to

its banks with rushing black water—the source of the gurgling noise they had heard in the tunnel. The river was much too wide for any of the Olympians to attempt leaping across it, except for maybe Hermes if she had a running start.

Ares ran up to the riverbank and began lapping up the water noisily—then immediately spat it out. "Yuck!" His eyes flashed red, and he shook off his tongue. "I hate this! HATE IT!"

"What's your beef, buddy?" Hermes asked, startled.

Athena stared at Ares suspiciously. "Yeah, you usually love anything that fits in your mouth."

Ares's eyes faded to normal, but his expression was dazed. "I … I don't know what got into me. For a second there, I just felt so *angry*." He stared at the dark current. "Something in the water."

"The water," Athena repeated. "The raging water marking the entrance to the Underworld. This must be the River Styx, from the Oracle's lesson."

The Olympians looked downstream for a bridge or another way to cross. The only landmark nearby was a round boulder on their side of the riverbank, about as large as Poseidon's dive helmet.

"This'll be a quick visit if we can't figure out a way to cross it," Hermes said.

"You seek to cross the Styx?" said a gravelly voice.

"Who said that?" Demeter demanded.

The other Olympians looked around.

"Is that you, Hades?" Poseidon asked.

"Didn't sound like Hades," Athena said.

"I'm not Hades," said the gravelly voice, "but you'll never get anywhere near him without my assistance."

The voice was coming from the round boulder on the riverbank. As the Olympians watched, the boulder unrolled itself into a four-legged creature with a body encased in rocklike scales.

"If this is the River Styx, would that make you Charon?" Athena asked the scaly creature, careful to pronounce it "Kah-run" like the Oracle did.

"I am the living ferry, yes." Charon's voice was surprisingly deep, considering his tiny mouth at the tip of his snoutlike head. The creature tumbled into the black water and bobbed on his back, his bulbous body making the perfect raft. He clutched a paddle. "If you wish to cross the Styx, you must pay the toll."

CHAPTER 14

THE OLYMPIANS WATCHED THE CREATURE propel himself to and fro with swishes of his scaly tail, easily keeping his position in the dark current. "You sure float good, Charon," Ares said. "Maybe you should change your name to Bob."

"Lemme handle this," Athena whispered to Ares. "Okay, Charon, what's the toll?"

Charon swam to the riverbank and crawled ashore, where he rose up on his hind legs to address the Olympians. "Those who seek a ride on Charon the living ferry must pay a toll of ..." He paused dramatically, letting the echoes of his deep voice fade. "... TWO OBOLS!" Charon's beady eyes regarded each Olympian. The pointy ears on his head twitched.

"Ooh, that's a bargain!" Ares exclaimed. He sat up on

78

his stocky behind and patted down his fur with his front paws, hunting for payment. A tiny stash of Mutt Nuggets dropped from his collar. The remnant of a well-chewed rawhide flopped from a wrinkle of fur behind a shoulder. Ares took stock of his loot, then scrunched up his face. "Wait. What's an obol?"

"It's a Greek coin," Poseidon said, his voice full of contempt. He turned to face the boatman. "How dare you charge the lord of all water to cross his own realm."

"Your realm doesn't extend to the Underworld, sea lord," the creature said. "The River Styx belongs to—hey!" Charon squeaked as Poseidon suddenly brushed past.

He stopped at the river's edge, examining the dark water. "Athena, you've done a fine job leading us until now, but I believe the current situation falls under my particular expertise."

"Aye." Athena nodded.

Charon seemed about to protest, but Poseidon didn't stick around. He rolled his helmet into the river, disappearing at once beneath the dark current.

CHAPTER 15

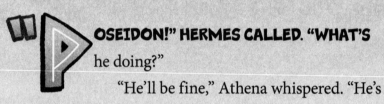OSEIDON!" HERMES CALLED. "WHAT'S
he doing?"

"He'll be fine," Athena whispered. "He's
in his element. Literally."

The Olympians and Charon watched the surface for
any sign of Poseidon. All they saw was his lifeline
steadily moving in the water. Soon, even the lifeline
stopped moving.

Charon turned from the river and glowered at the
Olympians, his tiny mouth smirking. "Your sea lord is
in over his head. Now he's just a soul lost to the River
Styx, like many others before him. Anyone else wish to
follow him?"

Athena kept her eyes on the unmoving lifeline.

"Should we maybe try to pull Poseidon out by his hose thingy?" Hermes suggested.

"You will do no such thing," Charon commanded. "Your sea lord refused to pay my price to cross the River Styx. Now he is paying the ultimate price."

"We can't just leave Poseidon down there!" Demeter exclaimed.

Athena's face lit up. "Olympians, look—the river!"

The rushing current of the river had slowed, at least by half, the black water less turbulent. Not only that, the water level had begun to drop, exposing more of the rocky bank. The River Styx was draining before their eyes! Within a minute, it was more like a creek than a raging river.

Charon stared in disbelief. "How ... how is this possible?"

"There he is! Poseidon!" Demeter pointed upstream to the crack in the cavern wall from which the river seemed to flow. The top of Poseidon's helmet was visible now that the river was draining around it. They could see Poseidon inside, puffed up to the capacity of his habitat. He had wedged his helmet into a large, round

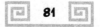

pipe protruding from the cavern wall just above the river bottom. Water continued to flow around his helmet and below it, but it was just a trickle, barely an inch deep. Poseidon had plugged up the source of the River Styx.

Demeter shook her head in wonder. "Cunning move, Poseidon."

The pufferfish calmly turned in his helmet toward the Olympians watching him from the riverbank. "Now would be a good time to cross."

Leaving Charon flabbergasted, they all slid down the wet rock and dashed across the soggy muck of the river bottom, splashing in the puddles and the slow trickle that remained of the drained River Styx.

They were barely halfway across when Charon recovered from his shock. "That's ... that's cheating!" Charon sputtered as he coiled once again into his boulder shape and rolled down the steep riverbank— straight toward Poseidon.

"Don't dally, friends," Poseidon warned. "I can't stop up this river forever."

Demeter and Hermes had reached the opposite riverbank. *CRACK!* They turned just in time to see

Charon smack into Poseidon like a cue ball. "Take that, you cheating cheater!" Charon screamed.

Poseidon's helmet was knocked from its spot. Water erupted from the pipe in a torrent. The full force of the River Styx was rushing toward Athena and Ares as they struggled up the slick rocks.

"Hurry!" Hermes yelled.

"Jump!" Demeter screamed.

Both Athena and Ares leapt ashore just a moment

before the river swept behind them.

"Anyone see Poseidon?" Demeter asked.

"Or Charon?" Hermes added.

The Olympians sat in tense silence, their eyes darting across the roiling surface. Ares plopped down and began licking the river muck off his paws. "Rahhh!" he bellowed. His eyes had become angry red pits inside his Spartan war helmet.

"Ares, quit licking river stuff!" Athena yelled.

The pug tucked his tail and whimpered as his eyes returned to normal.

SPLISH! A bulbous shape had popped up just offshore. Black water roiled around it, making it hard to tell if it was Charon or Poseidon in his helmet. The shape rolled up the riverbank. The Olympians held their breath.

"I told that Charon fellow this was my realm," came a familiar voice. The pufferfish gave a triumphant smile to his fellow Olympians. He had deflated back to his normal size.

There was still no sign of Charon. The guardian of the Styx had washed away in his own river.

"This is no time for a beach picnic," Poseidon said, raising his trident and pointing toward a path leading deeper into the vast Underworld. "Onward to the Cap of Shadows."

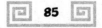

CHAPTER 16

BACK ON MOUNT OLYMPUS, ZEUS PACED IN his palace. He was developing a maddening routine. Each time he reached the western side, he peered down nervously at the closed portal to uncharted territory. Each time he reached the eastern side, he scowled at the three-headed hound standing guard over Greece in his doghouse.

Zeus worried for his fellow Olympians, who were trapped in uncharted territory—and attempting a dangerous mission—without his leadership. Seeing Cerberus filled him with frustration. The white patch on his cheek twitched with every step. Zeus stopped by his food bowl and grabbed a few morsels of Fuzzy Feast, hoping a snack might calm his nerves.

It didn't. He felt cooped up. Helpless. Alone. Finally, he couldn't stand it anymore. Zeus ran to the eastern edge of his palace and banged on the pillars with his fists. "You can't keep me in here like some rat in a cage," Zeus raged. "I'm Zeus the Mighty!"

Cerberus ignored him.

"Look," Zeus said, popping another piece of Fuzzy Feast into his mouth, "you seem like a reasonable monster dog. You don't want to be here. And it just so happens that I don't want to be here, either. How about we just go our separate ways?"

Cerberus didn't acknowledge him.

Zeus tried again. "Maybe we can make a deal. I bet your belly's starting to grumble without your boss, Hades, to feed you." Zeus paused. "Hey, do you have three bellies to go with your three heads?"

Nothing from Cerberus.

"It's not important. Anyway, how about you let me out for just a few hours, and I'll bring you back a big bowl of Mutt Nuggets fresh from the sack to fill that empty belly—er, bellies?—of yours?"

Silence.

"Three bowls!" Zeus added, spitting bits of Fuzzy Feast. "One for each head!"

The doghouse continued to scan Greece.

"I'm talking to you, fleabag!" Zeus threw his last crumb at Cerberus. It bonked off the roof of his hut, but Cerberus didn't react.

"You don't care what I do," Zeus pouted, "as long as I don't leave." He might as well have been talking to himself. Cerberus kept scanning to and fro, ignoring him. "Don't mind me, then." Zeus stomped angrily to the wall at the rear of the palace. "I'll just be over here plotting my escape."

Zeus examined the enchanted artifacts he kept on his back wall, trying to find something useful. He paused at the empty spot where the aegis once hung. It was a shield that doubled as a grappling hook, which would've come in handy now if he hadn't lost it to a conniving Harpy. Zeus shook his head and moved on to Hekate's torch. It was a tube-shaped relic that projected a piercing magical light in dark places. "Ares goes crazy chasing the beam from this thing. I bet a dog who lives in the dark would love it even more."

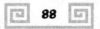

Zeus pulled the torch off the wall and tucked it under his arm. He aimed the crystal on its tip toward Cerberus's house, then pressed the rubber nub on the torch's side. *CLICK*. A beam of blinding light streamed from the mountaintop palace to the doghouse.

Zeus wiggled the torch under his arm, making the light dance in wild circles outside Cerberus's front door. "Get it, Cerby! Fetch the light, fetch the light!"

Cerberus didn't react.

"You're no fun!" Zeus said, wiggling Hekate's torch even harder. "Ares would be all over that!"

He sighed. "At least let me see what you look like in there!" He aimed the beam directly into the guard dog's entryway, hoping to get a glimpse of the three-headed hound within. Yet the light didn't penetrate the portal's dark depths. "What Underworld magic is this?" Zeus wondered, growing frustrated. It was almost as if some spell blocked the light from entering Cerberus's domain.

"So much for that bright idea," Zeus fumed. He dropped the torch on the palace floor.

CHAPTER 17

"**WHICH WAY?" POSEIDON ASKED** again. The Olympians had arrived at a crossroads not far from the River Styx, which they could still hear raging behind them and to the west.

The road split to the north, the south, and straight ahead due east. The path north disappeared into a series of gentle hills from which two rivers cascaded down jagged rocks in several treacherous waterfalls. The road south led into a thick forest of mushrooms sprouting around a vast lake of thick black water that looked like tar. The road east snaked downhill along a gnarled tree root and into a lowland shrouded in fog.

"Maybe we could split up," Hermes offered.

"No!" Demeter objected. "We don't have time to go traipsing all over the Underworld. The Cap is in the House of Hades. Let's just put our heads together and find the place."

"Why don't we ask for directions?" Ares suggested.

"Ask who?" Demeter leaned her two front legs on an exposed tree root. "The only Underworldling we met so far tried to drown us."

"The snake," Ares answered as if it were obvious.

"Snake?" Demeter looked around. "What snake?"

"The one you're sitting on," Ares said.

The gnarled root beneath Demeter began to shift. "Aaahh!" She leapt atop Poseidon's helmet.

Everyone except Ares shrank back as the root, which must have been five feet long, slowly wrapped around itself. Soil fell off its sides as it slithered, revealing scales that were a deep blue—indigo to be precise. The scales reflected the green light from high above.

The snake lifted its head over its coiled body and regarded the Olympians with eyes the color of the sea at midnight, that were barely visible among the black scales. A long forked tongue flicked from the dark line of its mouth, tasting the air.

"You couldn't have told us about the snake sooner?!" Demeter shouted.

"I thought it was obvious." Ares shrugged.

"How did you know that root was a snake to begin with?" Hermes asked him.

"He smelled like a snake." Ares snuffled. "Take a whiff. Classic snake."

Hermes recoiled. "I'll take your word for it, buddy."

"Apologies, newcomers." The snake's voice was deep, clear, soothing—hardly snakelike. "I meant no deception or harm. I was merely enjoying a relaxing hibernation when you came upon me." Its eyes flashed to gold before returning to indigo.

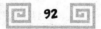

CHAPTER 18

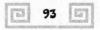O ONE SPOKE OR MOVED. THE OLYMPIANS stood transfixed by the snake, especially the reptile's odd eyes, which pulsed slowly from gold to indigo.

All except Hermes. She scanned her fellow Olympians in confusion, wondering what captivated them. Thinking everyone was seeing something extraordinary in the distance, she craned her head to look beyond the snake. But the snake moved to block Hermes's view, fixing the hen with his pulsing eyes. Finally, Hermes could no longer tolerate the awkward silence.

"Uh, sorry to stumble on ya like that, snake," she said. "We didn't mean to interrupt your nap."

The sound of Hermes's voice seemed to shake the Olympians out of their stupor, although they were still dazed.

"What's your name?" Athena asked the snake dreamily as she stretched out.

"I am Hypnos," the snake replied in his soothing voice, "son of the night, living embodiment of the River Lethe." Hypnos's eyes flared silver this time before fading to indigo.

"The River Lethe, huh?" asked Hermes warily. "That was the sleepy one from the Oracle's lesson, right?"

"Hypnos. That's a cool name," mumbled Ares in a soft, faraway voice.

Hermes noticed the pug swaying slightly on his feet, but before she could ask about it, he plopped down on his belly. All the other Olympians were on the ground, too. "What's up, y'all?" Hermes asked.

"Anyone ever tell you that you have a most comforting presence, Hypnos?" Poseidon asked, his eyelids drooping.

"It's his voice." Ares yawned, stretching his legs in front of him. His tongue flopped out. "Listening to him

is like lying in a sunbeam on a cold day—except in my brain."

"What?!" Hermes sputtered.

"No, no," Demeter protested. "It's his eyes. They're just so … so …" Her mouth hung open.

"I really think we should be moving along," Hermes shouted, trying to rally the squad. No one budged.

"I do get these sorts of compliments a lot," Hypnos replied. His head bobbed gently left and right, left and right, while his eyes flared gold again. "I suppose it's why I'm so good at my job."

"And what job is that?" Hermes snapped. "Nappin' in the dirt?"

"Hibernation is not a job—it's a way of life down here," Hypnos said. "I encourage all new residents of the Underworld to try it." His head kept bobbing, and his eyes pulsed from gold to silver.

"Don't mind if I do," Demeter said dreamily, her antennae drooping.

Poseidon, Ares, Athena, and Demeter were all on the verge of falling asleep. "We're not new residents," Hermes insisted, now really worried. "We're just visiting. And now we really need to be going!"

Hypnos bobbed his head closer to Hermes, his eyes cycling faster. "No one just visits the Underworld—anyone who crosses the River Styx never leaves. I simply help them pass the time." He bobbed closer so that his forked tongue flicked just inches from Hermes's beak.

"I don't know who you're trying to impress with your slick voice and flashy eye trick," Hermes scoffed, "but it ain't working on us. Right, everyone?"

When she turned back to the Olympians, she found her friends all frozen somewhere between asleep and awake. They stared into space, still as statues.

CHAPTER 19

"**Y**'ALL! Y'ALL, WAKE UP!" HERMES pleaded. She tried yelling, "Olympians, assemble!" in their faces. She waved her wings in front of Poseidon, but he floated listlessly in his mobile habitat, his three-pronged crown askew. His trident had fallen to the bottom of his dive helmet.

"What'd you do to them?!" Hermes demanded of Hypnos.

The snake answered in his maddeningly calm voice, "My job." He was still weaving left and right, his eyes strobing.

"Again with the job!" Hermes accidentally stepped on Ares's tongue, but the pug didn't even stir. "How's *this* a job?" She waved to her stupefied fellow Olympians.

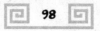

"As I explained, I welcome newcomers to the Underworld," the snake answered. "I help them make the most of their new lives."

"I don't know what that means," Hermes snapped, "but it doesn't sound good!"

Instead of answering, Hypnos again bobbed his head closer to Hermes and continued his rhythmic dance, his eyes shifting from gold to silver.

"Will you knock that off?!" Hermes shoved Hypnos.

"How can you resissst me?" Hypnos hissed, suddenly sounding snakelike.

"Whatever you're tryin' to do to me ain't doin' what it's doin' to them!" Hermes replied. "I'm Hermes, the Greek deity of sleep, you know! The master of zonk! When Greeks want sweet dreams, they pray to me! If anyone has the ticket to dreamland here, you're lookin' at her!" Hermes puffed out her chest and put her wings on her hips. "Now wake up my friends, or I will!"

Hypnos stared back blankly, but he'd halted his annoying dance. And his eyes had returned to indigo. "Sleep is the only escape from the Underworld." Hypnos almost sounded sad. "If you insist on waking your

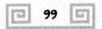

friends, you will be subjecting them to an eternity of Hades's cruel rule. And if that's the case, then you can all go kneel before his throne!" Hypnos writhed in the dirt, covering his scales with soil. In seconds, he was stretched to his full five-foot length, in the same pose as when the Olympians mistook him for a root.

Hermes barely noticed. Hypnos's words rang through her head."Hades's throne? That's exactly where we want to go! Stay awake, snake!" she squawked at Hypnos. "I have one more question before I break my buddies out of your spell: Where is the House of Hades?"

Hypnos didn't respond. Hermes feared the snake had already slipped back into hibernation, but just as his eyes closed, he whispered something.

"Say again!" Hermes yelled, running the length of Hypnos's body to address his head. "Where is it?"

"That way," Hypnos hissed, flicking his tongue toward the south.

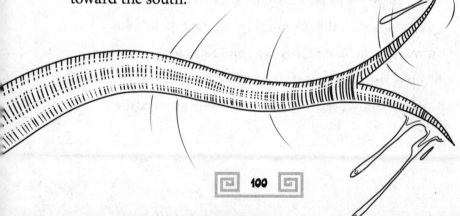

CHAPTER 20

ERMES LOOKED SOUTH. ALL SHE SAW WAS
a path leading into a mushroom forest. "Well,
I sure ain't goin' to Hades's house solo. Time
for the gang to rise and shine." She cleared her throat
and threw back her head. "Brach-crock-a-doodle-doooo!"

But Hermes's singing was swallowed by the thick air
of the Underworld. Her frozen friends hadn't moved.

"Hrmm. That usually wakes anyone who ain't dead."
Hermes ruffled her feathers with concern. "Must be the
terrible acoustics down here." She cleared her throat
again and reared back for another attempt, this time
putting more oomph into it. "BRACH-CROCK-A-
DOODLE-DOOOO!" Her song carried farther but was
again absorbed into the glowing moss on the ceiling.

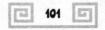

Her fellow Olympians still hadn't stirred.

"C'mon, now, sleep and wakefulness are part of my godly jurisdiction," Hermes said to herself. "Maybe my powers don't work down here?" Looking around, she spotted some low-lying cliffs, their faces sheer, that would create a natural amplifier. "I need to boost the volume on my wake-up call." She faced the cliffs and threw back her head. "BRACH-CROCK-A-DOODLE-DOOOO!" she belted with all her might. She had never crowed so loud before. But most of her song still sounded muted—except to the north, where it echoed loudly off the cliff faces.

Hermes was distraught to see that the Olympians remained frozen. With her heart pounding, she began mustering the strength for one final attempt when Athena suddenly bolted upright. "Where's ... where's the snake?" she asked groggily.

Hermes clapped her wings together in relief. "Athena, you're awake!"

"Was ... was I asleep?" the cat asked weakly. She looked at Ares, Poseidon, and Demeter, all still zonked out. "What's with them?"

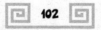

"Hypnos," Hermes said, pointing at the root lying nearby. "He did some kind of voodoo with his eyes ... or maybe his voice. Or both. Said he wanted to send y'all to dreamland forever." She looked at Ares, Demeter, and Poseidon, who were finally starting to stir. "Help me get these lazybones moving."

Athena, still dazed by Hypnos's spell, shook her head and whispered into Ares's ear: "Breakfast time!"

"Wha?!" Ares pushed himself to his feet, wide awake. "Where?!" he barked. He darted forward and tripped over his tongue, landing in a clumsy roll that sent his helmet tumbling.

Poseidon blinked sleep out of his eyes as he reached blindly around the bottom of his habitat, feeling for his trident. Finally, his fin closed on it and he straightened his crown. "I ... I seem to have nodded off. How rude of me." He eyed the rootlike form beside them suspiciously.

Demeter yawned. "Five more minutes, please, Zeus?" she mumbled. "Then I'll be ready for tonight's adventure." Her eyes drooped back shut.

Hermes laughed. "Zeus ain't here, Demeter. *You're* in charge of tonight's adventure, remember?"

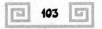

Demeter's eyes snapped open. "Right, right!" she said, suddenly alert. "We're off to borrow the Cap of Shadows." She tried to shake off Hypnos's hypnosis. "Last I remember Poseidon was leading us ..."

"Then we met that soothing snake," Ares continued. He had recovered his helmet and was now sniffing warily at Hypnos's rootlike body.

"Yep," Hermes said. "That soothing snake put y'all right to sleep. But I woke you back up. Guess it was my turn to lead."

"You had the resilience to resist Hypnos's spell," Athena said.

"Resilience was one of the qualities the Oracle said we'd need to reach the House of Hades," Demeter added.

"Which, by the way, I now know where to find," Hermes said proudly. "Hypnos told me while y'all were gettin' your beauty sleep." She strutted off to the south. "Everyone follow me."

The other Olympians, still a bit fuzzy-headed, stumbled into line behind her.

CHAPTER 21

ZEUS WAS STARING AT HIS WALL OF
magical artifacts again. Hekate's torch had
been a bust. The aegis shield was missing. All
he had left were the tatters of the Nemean cloak. It was
made from the hide of a legendary lion. Whoever wore
the cloak became invincible. Zeus unhooked it from the
wall and held it. Its fur looked ratty—but then again,
the cloak had been through a lot. Zeus had worn it to
vanquish the Hydra monster. The cloak had nearly been
lost in that battle, until Hermes recovered it during her
trials to become a full-fledged Olympian.

Now Zeus wondered how it could help him with
Cerberus. "I need invisibility, not invincibility," he
grumbled. He threw it around his shoulders and pulled

the mane over his crown like a hood, the lion's face and whiskers resting atop Zeus's brow. The lion's raggedy tail dragged behind him.

It was a happy accident that the Nemean cloak was the perfect size for him. It was too small for Ares, Athena, or Hermes. Poseidon couldn't stomach the possibility of any fur floating around in his habitat. And, of course, the cloak was much too large for Demeter. "Too large for Demeter …" Zeus repeated his thought out loud, and a smile crept up his face. He had a new escape plan.

Minutes later, Zeus admired his handiwork. "Hello, handsome," he said to a life-size replica of himself that he'd stitched together from the Nemean lion cloak. It stood on legs made from sticks and was stuffed with straw-like material Zeus had scavenged from the floor of his palace. He'd wrapped his replica in a spare chiton

pinned with a crude copy of his thunderbolt badge. He'd even fashioned a golden laurel of thread ripped from his fleece bed and set it atop the lion's head to help tame its mane. To finish it off, he re-created the white cloud patch on his cheek with a piece of bed stuffing.

"It's like looking in a mirror!" Zeus marveled. *POP!* One of the eyes he'd molded from a piece of Fuzzy Feast fell to the floor. Zeus picked it up and hurriedly stuck it back on the dummy Zeus. "Keep it together, Zeus Deuce. I need you to distract old Six-Eyes out there."

Zeus grunted as he dragged his dummy to the palace wall closest to Cerberus. He propped it against the pillars of his palace and wiggled one of its arms to get Cerberus's attention. "Hey, poochy! Check me out!" Zeus yelled, crouching behind his clone. But the portal to Cerberus's guard hut remained dark. "Oh, right." Zeus slapped his forehead. "Cerberus only seems to care if I leave my palace."

It took some time to cram the dummy between two pillars—its straw stuffing kept squeezing out in the process. But as soon as Zeus propped it against the outside of the palace, Cerberus's flashing red eyes

materialized. Zeus began waving the replica's stick arms again. "Look who's out and about, Mr. Mutt!" he yelled. "Ahhh, how about that fresh air?!"

"Woof! Woof! Woof!" Cerberus barked in alarm. Its white and purple eyes also pivoted in Zeus's direction, alerted by the first head's barking.

"Cerberus is smitten," Zeus whispered. "Now's my chance." He sprinted toward the back of the palace and his secret exit. But before he was even halfway there, Cerberus went quiet. Zeus glanced back and saw that the guard dog's eyes had gone dark.

"Drat!" Zeus muttered. "I suppose I need to make Zeus Deuce a little livelier if I'm going to keep the pup's attention." He plopped down in his exercise wheel, unsure what to do next. That's when he spotted the loose thread on his Golden Fleece bed.

Zeus leapt to his feet and began pulling out the thread.

CHAPTER 22

"**Y**OU'RE SURE THE HOUSE OF HADES IS this way?" Demeter asked as the Olympians trekked south.

"That's what the snake said." Hermes was leading them uphill through the mushroom meadow.

"You know, Hypnos is one of Hades's cronies." Athena looked warily at the mushrooms that stretched in all directions. "I smell a trick."

"Probably." Demeter shrugged. "But right now it's our only lead."

"What's a trick even smell like?" Ares sniffed. "All I smell is animals."

"What animals?" Hermes looked around.

"Those ones." Ares waved at some mushrooms.

The Olympians turned to examine the thick forest of mushrooms that sprouted just a few inches off their path. The longer they stared, the more obvious it became that these weren't normal mushrooms—or even mushrooms at all.

Poseidon was inspecting a particularly stout mushroom. "Are my eyes playing tricks, or is that mushroom a guinea pig?"

"Is this one an owl?" Athena asked.

"This one looks like a cricket," Demeter said, brushing dirt off a mushroom near her.

"Close. I'm a mole cricket," the mushroom replied in a high-pitched voice, shaking off more dirt and coming to life before everyone's eyes.

"Oh, sorry!" Demeter recoiled in surprise and stared wide-eyed at her fellow insect. She was Demeter's size but with stubbier legs and an armored body. From one antenna dangled a small, wilted flower with vibrant yellow petals. "Who are you?!" Demeter asked.

"I'm Persephone," the mole cricket said. Her voice was childlike. "I'm the leader of the Underworldlings." She waved at the mushrooms.

The Olympians realized that an entire zoo's worth of animals—dirty with dust and soil—spread before them posing as mushrooms.

"What's with this place?" Hermes shook her head. "First a snake disguised as a tree root, and now all these animals pretending to be mushrooms."

"I'm sure Demeter could explain it," Persephone said, shooting Demeter a sly smile. "Of course she knows that the snake is responsible for all of this. I mean, she's the great Demeter, the mightiest Olympian!"

Demeter blushed. She was glad Zeus wasn't here to balk at the cricket's compliment. "I'm not sure everyone would agree with you on that, Persef ... Persef-oh-nee?" Demeter took care to pronounce her name.

"Oh, you're so humble. That's classic Demeter!" Persephone hooted. "Everyone in the Bugcropolis knows you're the greatest Olympian! We hear it from

the time we're itty-bitty larvae!"

"The Bugcropolis?" Athena interrupted. "You're from Demeter's hometown?"

"Yeah, but I left it to see the world, just like my hero." The cricket smiled at Demeter. "Though, I didn't end up becoming an Olympian like Demeter." She paused, twitching an armored leg. "I took a pretty big wrong turn, actually. Found my way down here under that sneaky snake's spell, just like the other Underworldlings."

"How long have you all been here?" Athena asked.

"Oh, I don't know. Months? Years?" Persephone fiddled absentmindedly with the flower on her antenna. Several yellow petals fell to the ground. "But now it doesn't matter! Demeter has come to lead us all out of here!" She grinned adoringly at Demeter.

The grasshopper squirmed. "Um, sure, we can totally"—Demeter noticed Athena frantically shaking her head no—"look into it."

Persephone's grin faded. "Look into it?"

Athena stepped between Demeter and Persephone. "Excuse us," she told the mole cricket as she pulled Demeter into a huddle with the other Olympians.

CHAPTER 23

IHATE TO STEP ON YOUR BUGCROPOLIS reunion," Athena whispered to Demeter as the other Olympians leaned in to hear, "but I'm not so sure becoming the leader of an army of Underworldlings is the best idea right now."

Demeter scanned the field of zonked animals sprawling into the distance and imagined the chaos they would create if Hermes woke them up. "Actually, they might be just the help our mission needs."

"Mission? What mission?" Persephone called from several feet away. The Olympians gaped at her. "Oh, apologies. I didn't mean to eavesdrop," she explained. "It's just we mole crickets have really good hearing."

"That must be why my crowin' woke you up but not the other Underworldlings," Hermes mused. "You've got, like, supersenses."

Persephone turned to Hermes excitedly. "You have the power to break the snake's spell?"

"You're awake, ain't ya?" Hermes shrugged.

"Of course Demeter brought just the right Olympians to rescue us!" Persephone gushed. "I shouldn't be surprised!"

Demeter nibbled thoughtfully at the lettuce sash on her shoulder. "Honestly, Persephone, rescuing you wasn't part of our plan. We didn't even know about you Underworldlings until now." Persephone's face fell. Another petal tumbled from her flower.

Demeter pressed on. "But I'm glad we found you! I'm beginning to think you all could be a tremendous help with our mission."

Athena gave Demeter a funny look but said nothing.

"Again with this mission," Persephone said. "What are you up to?"

"We're gonna heist Hades's Hat of Hiding!" Ares blurted.

"Why didn't you say so?!" Persephone exclaimed. "Hades is such a big bully. That scary thunder." The mole cricket shuddered.

"We're headed to Hades's house," Hermes added. "We were told it's this way." She pointed south.

"You're not far!" Persephone cried. "I can take you!"

Before anyone could respond, Persephone scurried down a path. The Olympians hurried after her.

Soon enough, the group came to a pool at the base of a waterfall.

"Uh-oh. Dead end!" Ares yelled so he could be heard over the tumbling water. "I don't think I can climb those." He peered up at the cliffs surrounding the falls.

"Me neither," Demeter agreed. She turned to Persephone, who was waiting at the pool's edge. "You're sure the House of Hades is this way?"

"The front door is just beyond this wall of water," said the mole cricket as she inspected the waterfall. "But I'm allowed no farther. Underworldlings are forbidden from entering the House of Hades."

Poseidon moved closer to the waterfall. He hesitated for a moment, then continued rolling. His helmet disappeared beneath the pool's roiling surface, but his lifeline continued to spool in behind him.

Ares bowed low on his front legs, sniffing at the water. "Hey, sea lord! You okay down there?"

"Of course I'm okay," came Poseidon's voice. "I'm at Hades's front door."

"Where are you?" Demeter called.

"Here!" Poseidon shouted. "Follow the edge of the pool and you'll find me!"

The Olympians spotted a narrow path behind the waterfall. It led to a hidden grotto. Demeter turned back to the mole cricket, who hadn't moved. "Thanks for the tip, Persephone. We'll take it from here!"

"Wait! What about waking up the Underworldlings?"

"Patience, cricket," Demeter promised. "Waking them up is all part of the plan. Just go back to the meadow and hang tight."

"Okay. But be careful around Hades. He has all sorts of spooky powers." She paused, then remembered herself. "Oh, who am I talking to? The great Demeter can handle anything!" Persephone scurried away in the direction they had come from.

Athena turned to Demeter. "What exactly do you have in mind for the Underworldlings?"

Demeter shrugged. "It seems like they might be the only folks down here we can trust. If Hades uses more than just Cerberus to guard his magic cap, we're going to need some help."

Athena nodded.

"Are you all coming or not?" Poseidon's complaint carried loudly over the rushing water.

Carefully treading along the rocks, one by one the Olympians followed Demeter behind the waterfall.

CHAPTER 24

THE OLYMPIANS FOUND POSEIDON WAITING for them in a cold, misty grotto. He was peering into a grate where the pooling water drained. "I wonder which of the five rivers this is?" he asked.

"Maybe Ares can give it a taste test?" Demeter suggested.

"I could use a drink!" Ares lapped at the water, then swished it around in his mouth, gauging its flavor.

"What's it taste like, pal?" Hermes asked.

"It tastes like …" Ares scrunched his already wrinkly face. "Ack!" He spit out the water.

"Tastes like 'ack'?" Hermes saw that Ares's eyes had turned a sickly yellow. He looked on the verge of losing his lunch.

After a second, his face unscrunched and his eyes returned to normal.

"You said it tastes like 'ack,' right?" Athena asked. "This must be the River Ack-ur-run," she said, carefully pronouncing the name.

"Acheron," Demeter repeated, "the river of misery."

"Yeah, I was feeling pretty miserable," Ares muttered, although he looked like his chipper self again.

Hermes scratched Ares behind his ear. "Good thing you have that unbeatable belly, buddy."

"If this is the River Acheron," Athena reasoned, "that really must be the front door of the House of Hades." She pointed a paw toward a dim opening at the rear of the grotto. Demeter hopped through it first. The rest of the Olympians filed behind her. They found themselves in a larger cavern with smooth walls and a moss-lined floor. The roar of the waterfall faded.

"Somehow I thought Hades's house would be snazzier," Hermes said.

"Feels nice on my tootsies, though," Ares answered, flexing his paws on the mossy ground.

"I don't like how it pulls at my lifeline," Poseidon said

nervously. He was having a hard time moving his habitat through the moss.

"Ignore the decor," Demeter commanded. "Let's go find Hades's throne room, grab the Cap of Shadows, and get out of here."

The Olympians kept moving until they found their way blocked by a massive mound. At its top, a large tortoise shell sat wedged between the mound and the ceiling.

"Ungggg."

"Ares, keep a lid on that belly of yours," Athena hissed. "We're trying to be sneaky, remember?"

"That wasn't me," Ares protested, cocking an ear. "It came from inside that shell." The tortoise shell had begun to shimmy slightly. But then it settled down again. Whatever lived inside had gone still.

Demeter held a leg to her mouth, gesturing for silence. She pointed to a portal on the far side of the mound. They were nearly there when—*ting!*—a strange new sound rang out.

Demeter froze, and the Olympians bumped into her. All except Poseidon, whose habitat had stopped moving halfway across the room. His lifeline hung taut between him and the cavern's entrance.

"Apologies," Poseidon said sheepishly. "I seem to be having an issue here." He swam with all his might against the inside of his dive helmet. It bounced, making a *TING, TING, TING* sound, but it didn't budge. "Ahem … well, it appears I've reached the end of my lifeline. First time that's ever happened."

Before anyone could respond, the tortoise shell atop the mound began shimmying again. This time, four wrinkly legs and a head with a blunt snout and large, expressive eyes emerged.

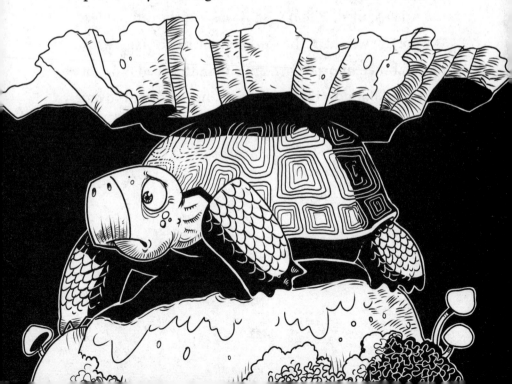

"Oh, thank the gods!" the tortoise exclaimed in his deep, slow voice. "I thought I heard someone messing around out there. I never dreamed the Olympians would come to rescue me!"

"Rescue you ... from what?" Demeter asked suspiciously. "Who are you?"

"The name's Atlas," the tortoise replied. "I've been stuck between this rock and hard place for as long as I can remember, holding this up." He wiggled a foot toward the cavern ceiling that seemed to rest on his back.

"Holding up the ceiling?" Athena asked.

Atlas scoffed. "Oh, I wish it was just the ceiling! No, I've got the weight of the world on my back." His narrow mouth broke into a bigger smile than they had thought possible. "But now that you're here, my torment is over!"

CHAPTER 25

ZEUS'S ARMS ACHED, BUT HE COULDN'T GIVE up now. He'd spent the past 20 minutes spooling the thread around his forearm. He estimated he had at least five feet. "That ought to be enough." He bit the end of it to separate it from the Golden Fleece piece. "At least I hope so."

Zeus carried the thread over to the dummy he'd made. "What's new, Zeus Deuce?"

It lay right where he'd left it, practically beneath the nose of the three-headed hound. But Cerberus never noticed it because it was motionless. That was about to change.

Zeus pulled his clone back into the palace and dragged it toward the southern edge, which overlooked

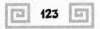

all of Greece. He tied one end of his thread around the dummy's waist, and the other end to a rung on his exercise wheel. Satisfied the thread was secure, Zeus stepped into his wheel and began walking briskly.

As he walked, the thread wrapped around the wheel. Zeus could see it would take a while to wind the entire thing, so he picked up the pace.

"I ... I really hope Demeter and the Olympians appreciate ... all the exercise I'm getting to rescue them," Zeus said, panting. And yet he ran faster, occasionally glancing over toward the portal to uncharted territory, which remained shut.

CHAPTER 26

THE OLYMPIANS HUDDLED TOGETHER
watching Atlas squirm in his stuck shell.

"Do you think we can trust him?" Demeter
whispered.

"I don't trust anyone down here." Athena eyed
Atlas warily.

"We trusted Persephone," Ares pointed out. "This
guy seems like he's in the same bind, trapped in the
Underworld against his will. Maybe he's a part of
her crew?"

"Yeah, but Persephone was out in the wilds of the
Underworld," Hermes said. "This fella appears to be a
houseguest of Hades's!"

"What are my heroes talking about down there?"

Atlas called down, his legs dangling uselessly.

"We're wondering if we can trust you," Ares blurted.

The other Olympians cringed. "Of course you can trust me!" Atlas said. "Wait, why wouldn't you trust me?"

"No offense," Hermes said, "but most of the folks down here seem to work for Hades."

"Pahhh!" Atlas scoffed. "I've no loyalty to Hades—he's the one who put me here!" Atlas wiggled his legs again to illustrate his predicament.

"Hades did this to you?" Athena asked. "Why?"

"Long story. I wouldn't want to bore you busy Olympians. But if you free me, I'll be happy to assist with whatever you're up to."

"I wish we could help, Atlas," Demeter said, "but we're under a lot of pressure right now."

"You don't have to tell me about pressure!" Atlas tapped a leg against his shell.

Poseidon puffed himself up in his helmet to get a better look at the tortoise. "Atlas, if we break you free, do you promise to take us directly to Hades's Cap of Shadows?"

"You want to find his invisibility cap? That's easy!"
the tortoise said. "It's in the throne room! I can get you
there a secret way!" He held up a leg. "Swear to gods!"

Poseidon raised his eyebrows at Demeter and
Athena. Both shrugged, as if to say, *Why not?*

Poseidon pointed his trident and called to Ares.
"War god, mind using your head to knock our trapped
friend here free? That's step one."

Ares began spinning excitedly, Hippolyta's belt
jangling against his collar. "Ooh, ooh! I'll free you, Atlas!
I'll free you!" He clambered up the mound and butted

against Atlas with his Spartan war helmet. As Atlas started to move, the cavern ceiling began to quiver.

"What … what are you doing?!" the turtle exclaimed as he scraped against the stone. "My shell's the only thing holding up the world!" Dust and pebbles were raining down around them.

"Are we sure about this?" Athena asked. Ares just grunted as he kept shoving Atlas free. A spiderweb of cracks had formed, and a shower of debris rained down.

"I … I'm going to assume they're sure," Hermes decided, holding her wings above her head. A slab of rock slammed into the ground next to her.

"Now for step two! Gangway!" Poseidon sped right between the Olympians with determination in his eyes. He was rolling his helmet straight up the mound, and—just as the ceiling seemed about to collapse—maneuvered himself into Atlas's old spot. His lifeline was stretched to the limit, and now the god of the oceans was holding up the weight of the world. Or at least his mobile habitat was.

The rain of dust and pebbles slowed, then stopped. The Underworld became still again.

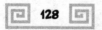

Athena called up
to Poseidon, "Good
thinking, sea lord."

"It was the end of the
line for me anyway—
literally," Poseidon replied.
"Now go get that silly cap!"

"Worry not," said Atlas. He
was walking in circles, marveling at being free again.
"Follow me, and you shall get all you deserve." Without
another word, the tortoise exited the chamber.

Ares trotted after him without hesitation. The other
Olympians looked back at Poseidon wedged under the
weight of the cavern ceiling.

"Bring a boulder or something to swap with me
when you come back," Poseidon called down. "I don't
intend to spend any more time holding up the world
than I have to."

The Olympians reluctantly headed after Atlas. "Hang
tight, sea lord!" Demeter said in farewell.

"Hang tight?" Poseidon muttered. "Where else would
I go?"

CHAPTER 27

ZEUS GAVE HIS PLAN ONE FINAL RUNDOWN.

"Spool?" Zeus eyed his exercise wheel, now wrapped in thread like a giant spool, and liked what he saw. "Check."

"Rope?" Zeus tugged, and the thread began unspooling slowly from the wheel. "Check." Then he spun the wheel in the opposite direction to respool what he'd just pulled free.

"Zeus Deuce?" He made his way to the southern edge of the palace and surveyed his substitute, which was propped against the palace pillars. The dummy's wooden limbs and stuffed lion cloak still held together. "Check!" Zeus clapped his clone on the back.

POP! One of his replica's Fuzzy Feast eyes had fallen

off again. Zeus managed to catch it before it tumbled over the edge of the palace. He stuck it back in place and smoothed out his clone's mane. "C'mon, Zeus Deuce, try to keep it together for just a few more minutes, will ya?"

Cerberus was keeping up his tireless duty watching over Greece.

"It's showtime, pal," Zeus said to his dummy. "Your job is to distract Cerberus, okay? Five minutes. That's all I need."

Zeus turned the dummy sideways and wedged it through the pillars. It hung off the edge of Mount Olympus, suspended over the void by the thread looped around its waist. Zeus clutched the thread with both paws, and started shaking it, making his clone sway.

"Woof! Woof! Woof!" Cerberus's red eyes flashed as he barked at the Zeus substitute. The other two heads joined in, their eyes flashing white and purple. Zeus kept at it until he was sure his clone had Cerberus's full attention.

"Have a good fall, buddy," Zeus said, releasing the rope. The dummy tumbled down, its limbs flopping.

The exercise wheel spun as it paid out the thread, controlling the clone's descent.

So far, the ruse was working—Cerberus was fixated on the falling dummy. He had stopped barking, but the eyes of all three heads were flashing.

"It's now or never," Zeus muttered. He bolted for the hidden gate at the back of his palace, expecting Cerberus's barking alert the moment he stepped out. Instead, the three-headed hound continued to ignore him.

Zeus didn't dare waste a moment to celebrate. He slid down the rope that led to the bottom of Mount Olympus and hit the ground running toward uncharted territory.

He skidded to a stop in front of the closed portal and risked a glance back toward his palace. Zeus Deuce was still falling slowly, and all three of Cerberus's heads were still fixated on it.

Zeus sat down to catch his breath and consider his options. The Olympians had recklessly allowed the portal to seal shut, and now he had to get it open. Quickly. His mind was racing for a solution when he noticed Athena's toy—the long stick with the fluffy feathers at one end—on the ground right next to the *Argo* in its dock. Zeus stroked the white patch on his cheek. "That might work," he said to himself.

CHAPTER 28

THE OLYMPIANS HAD BEEN FOLLOWING
Atlas for what seemed like ages through the
sprawling House of Hades, each room more
mind-blowing than the last. Now they came into a
circular chamber with a shallow pool of crystal-clear
water. A parched-looking field mouse dressed in
rags stood in the pool. The Olympians watched the
mouse cup his paws to take some water to drink, but
the pool drained beneath him. As soon as he pulled
his paws away from the water, the pool refilled. The
mouse's shoulders slumped, and he began the whole
process again.

"That's Tantalus the Thirsty," Atlas explained.
"He has a thirst curse—can't get any water to drink

no matter how much he tries.
Oh, mind your heads."

Atlas was already leading
them to the next chamber
through a portal partially
blocked by low-hanging moss.
Before he filed through, Ares
called back to Tantalus, "You probably
don't want to drink that water anyway! It'll just make
you sick or angry or something." But the mouse ignored
him, so Ares fell back into step with the others.

The next chamber was impossibly vast—one of its
long walls sloped upward like a rocky mountainside,
complete with a snow-capped peak. About halfway
up the slope, a massive dung beetle was grunting and
struggling to climb. He was so high that the Olympians
had to squint to make him out. The beetle was using
his hind legs to push an enormous rock—more of a
boulder, really—up the mountain. But the boulder
wouldn't budge.

"Sisyphus," Atlas declared, pointing at the beetle.
"Maybe someday he and that boulder will get up the

mountainside." They all watched as the beetle's footing gave way and the boulder rolled backward. "Or maybe not," Atlas said.

"I don't like this place," Hermes said. Her head shook.

"Remember this room," Demeter whispered to the other Olympians as they moved along. "We can use that beetle's boulder to free Poseidon later."

"I'm on it," Athena replied. She had made a point to leave a paw print at each portal they passed through.

Without Poseidon, they didn't have the benefit of his lifeline to lead them back the way they had come.

When they came to a cavern with hot iron pipes that crisscrossed the ceiling, the Olympians had to scramble and duck to avoid being singed.

"How much farther to the Cap?" Athena asked irritably as she shook out the tip of her tail which she had scalded on a pipe.

"Oh, it's not far now," Atlas answered with a strange glint in his eye. "You'll see. You'll all see."

The Olympians had no choice but to take his word

for it. Apart from noticing that they seemed to be heading slightly downhill, they had no way of knowing where they were.

And the air around them was growing colder and mistier. "If we go any farther into the Underworld," Ares said, "I'm going to need a fur coat."

"You have a fur coat," Hermes replied as she folded her wings tightly around her body. "So, Atlas," she said, "remind me again why you're helpin' us get the Cap?" Something about the tortoise made her uneasy.

"Oh, you'll see, you'll see," Atlas said again as they entered the largest cavern yet. "Ah, here we are."

"Here we are … where?" Demeter surveyed the chamber. Its round walls were perfectly smooth. The domed ceiling was covered with the same glowing green moss they'd seen earlier and more iron pipes. An arched portal yawned open at the far side of the room.

"You're just outside of Hades's throne room," Atlas said in a hushed tone. "Everything you deserve is here."

"The Cap of Shadows is here?" Hermes asked doubtfully.

"Guys, why's this ground so funky?" Ares was

shifting his paws nervously. They seemed to be sinking into the floor. "It's … like … eating me!"

"Ares, pull out your legs!" Demeter shouted. Lightest of the Olympians, she was able to float on top of the mucky ground, but her heavier comrades were becoming mired in it.

"This is a trap!" Athena announced. Her blue eyes narrowed, but she had already sunk to her fuzzy belly.

Before anyone could respond, the sandy floor collapsed beneath their feet, creating a deep pit in the center of the room. The Olympians tumbled into it— all except Hermes, who briefly pumped her wings and hovered in place before losing steam and joining the others.

Atlas looked down at them from the rim of the pit. "It's not a trap," the tortoise replied. "It's Tartarus. Your new home. Welcome." He disappeared from the edge and left them to their new fate.

CHAPTER 29

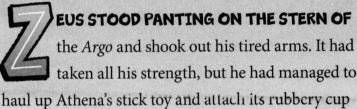EUS STOOD PANTING ON THE STERN OF
the *Argo* and shook out his tired arms. It had
taken all his strength, but he had managed to
haul up Athena's stick toy and attach its rubbery cup
to the deck at his feet. The *Argo* now had a flagpole.

He examined the vessel's controls, an assortment of
buttons and crystals. When Athena took the helm, she
knew exactly how to make the *Argo* do her bidding.

"Blast it, I wish I'd paid attention! Maybe this one?"
Zeus stepped on a crystal. *BOO-BERP.*

"CHARGE AT THIRTY PERCENT," the *Argo* said
in a robotic voice.

Zeus's shoulders slumped. "You and me both, *Argo*."
He glanced up at Mount Olympus. Zeus Deuce was

already halfway to the ground. The real Zeus needed to hurry.

"C'mon, *Argo*, giddyup!" He stepped on a larger silver button with strange markings—"POWER"—and the vessel's motor hummed to life. "Yes!" But the *Argo* remained docked.

"Move!" Zeus stepped on another button in frustration. *BOOP!* The *Argo* lurched backward away from the portal, rolling deeper into Greece.

"Wrong way! Wrong way!" Zeus frantically leapt on another button, and the ship reversed course, traveling straight for the portal to uncharted territory. "Okay, right direction," he muttered.

Zeus ran to the stern of the *Argo* and scrambled up Athena's stick. He grabbed the feather dangling from its top, then hung from it. The stick bent backward under his weight, just as Zeus hoped, and he dropped lower and lower behind the *Argo*. He braced himself for an impact.

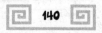

For a split second, Zeus turned his head and saw Zeus Deuce lying at the foot of Mount Olympus. Zeus also saw that Cerberus's portal was dark and it was panning across Greece again.

Then, *CRASH!* The *Argo* slammed into the portal to uncharted territory. *THWANG!* The sudden stop caused Athena's stick to recoil upward, catapulting Zeus to the knob he always saw Callie use to open the portal to uncharted territory.

Zeus had hoped to wrap his arms around the knob, but it was too large. As he slid down its side, though, he heard a *CLICK.* The portal popped open, and the stalled *Argo* started sailing through!

Zeus dropped onto its deck and landed with a roll. If he didn't stop the vessel, the portal would shut behind him. Then he'd be trapped with the Olympians he had come to rescue.

"All stop!" Zeus ordered, stepping on the round button. The *Argo*'s motor quieted, and the vessel stood wedged against the portal, holding it open.

Zeus flew off the bow, relieved to be out of Cerberus's gaze. He had a rescue mission to complete.

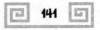

CHAPTER 30

"**Y'ALL OKAY?" HERMES FLAPPED WET** sand from her wings as she scanned the pit for her fellow Olympians.

"More or less," Athena answered from nearby. She shook grit from her whiskers. The deep sand at the pit's bottom had cushioned their fall, but the Olympians were a sorry, filthy sight.

Ares wiggled his meatloaf-shaped body, spraying soggy sand everywhere, while Demeter inspected their surroundings. She spotted a round metal plate bearing the image of a fish halfway up one of the sheer stone walls. In the dim green light, she could just make out a strange script running around its edges:

Hermes launched herself with a powerful thrust of her wings but barely made it halfway up before falling back to the floor. "I think we're stuck here," she said. She started pecking around the pit's perimeter.

"I can't believe Atlas led us here," Ares barked. "We tried to help him!"

"He used our Olympian mojo against us," Athena admitted. "Pretty cunning trick, actually."

"Do you think Persephone was leading us into a trap, too?" Ares asked. "I mean, can we trust anyone down here?"

"I trust Persephone," Demeter replied. "She and the Underworldlings aren't from around these parts."

"The tortoise called this place Tartarus," Athena said. "The Oracle's lesson described it as a prison not even a god could escape."

Demeter looked around. "Not one god, maybe," she said slowly, "but there are four of us. We have to be able to find a way out."

"Atlas called it our new home," Hermes added.

"That's not gonna work for me," Ares replied. "I don't have my bed or my bowl or Mutt Nuggets in my bowl." His belly growled, and he eyed Demeter's lettuce sash, now covered in sand. "Say, are you gonna eat that—"

KRAKOW! A thunderclap crashed upon them.

"Yippp!" Ares cowered beneath Hermes's wing like an oversize chick.

"You're wearin' Hippolyta's belt, buddy," the hen reminded him, pulling at the chain around Ares's collar. "It repels thunder, remember?"

Ares stuck his head out from beneath her wing. "Oh, yeah, th-that's right," he said timidly. "I … I forgot about that." He crawled back to his feet and shook, spraying Hermes with sand and slobber.

"It's not even real thunder anyway," Demeter said, trying to reassure Ares. "Zeus said there's something phony about it."

KRAKOW! Thunder cracked again, louder this time. It sounded like it came from directly over them.

"YIPPPPP!" Ares leapt back under Hermes's wing. "Sounds real to me," he whimpered.

The greenish light flickered as a light mist filtered down from above. "DID I OR DID I NOT WARN YOU TO STAY OUT OF MY REALM?!" Hades's deep voice boomed all around them.

The Olympians huddled in the pit. Ares piped up first. "Okay, we'll be happy to skedaddle. Do you have a ladder or something—"

KRAKOW! Ares jumped but held his ground this time. Hermes patted him with a wing.

"TOO LATE TO LEAVE NOW," Hades announced. "HERE YOU SHALL REMAIN, IN THE UNDERWORLD, FOREVER." And just like that, the fog above them faded. The pit brightened. Quiet settled back on Tartarus, their prison. Hades was gone.

CHAPTER 31

RES LOOKED DEJECTEDLY AT THE OTHER
Olympians. "Who wants to lead now?" he
asked, then immediately answered, "Not it!"

Athena plopped down and preened the silver tufts of
her ears. "There has to be some way out of this prison."

Hermes eyed the edge of the pit high above. "Ain't
prisons supposed to have bars?"

"Not sure this one needs them," Demeter answered.
"We can't climb out. You can't fly out. There's no way
Persephone would hear your singing way down here."
Her eyes again fell on the round plate halfway up the
wall. She stared at the fish in its center.

Demeter suddenly turned to Athena. "Would you
mind moving aside?"

"Okay." Athena shrugged and moved out of the center of the pit.

Demeter turned to Ares. "Buddy, you ready to flex that war-god brawn?"

"Aye!" Ares replied enthusiastically.

"I need you to dig us a hole right there." Demeter pointed where Athena had been sitting.

"On it!" Ares began scooping sand through his hind legs against the wall behind him.

"What's he digging for?" Athena asked, deftly springing out of the way of Ares's sand shower.

"Where there's fish, there's water," Demeter replied softly.

Athena looked up at the metal fish plate. "You might be on to something." She returned her attention to Ares in his rapidly expanding hole. "Dig, war god! Dig!"

Ares was making fast work of the sand. Hermes had joined in, scratching at the top of his hole to widen it. Soon, only Ares's stocky rump was visible, his curly tail waggling, as he dug deeper.

"Guys, something's down here!" Ares shouted. "Whoa!" His rump dropped from view. The Olympians heard a soft splash.

CHAPTER 32

ZEUS PEERED INTO THE GREEN DEPTHS OF the entrance to the Underworld. He had hoped that he would bash through the portal into uncharted territory and find his fellow Olympians waiting for him, Hades's hat in hand, thrilled that their king had opened their exit from this strange land.

But the only sign of them was Poseidon's lifeline, which trailed into the dimness. "At least they'll be easy to find." Zeus sighed and stepped into the Underworld.

He'd half expected Hades to welcome him with a show of thunder and mist, yet all remained quiet as Zeus wandered deeper into the cave. Roots coiled along the walls that narrowed into a tight tunnel. He ducked to avoid hitting his head on an overhang of white rock.

When he turned a corner and the tunnel opened before him, he couldn't believe his eyes. The Underworld sprawled before him, glittering in its odd green light.

But Zeus recovered from his awe and trekked onward, always following Poseidon's lifeline. When he came to the bank of a fast-moving river, he couldn't find any suitable places for him—or any of the Olympians—to cross: no shallows or stones or bridge of any kind. Yet Poseidon's lifeline stretched across it, nearly taut. Zeus leaned against a rock and stared at the opposite riverbank. "How in blazes did the Olympians get across this?"

"They cheated," answered the rock in a deep voice.

"Who?! Huh?!" Zeus shoved away from the boulder so hard that he had to windmill his arms to keep from tumbling to the muddy ground. He recovered his balance in time to watch the rock unfurl into a four-legged creature with a body encased in rocklike scales.

"I am Charon, the living ferry of the River Styx." The creature's voice echoed off the walls, and its tiny mouth fixed into a horrible smile revealing rows of pointed teeth. Charon tumbled into the river and floated on his back. "If you wish to cross, you must pay the toll."

Zeus stared dumbfounded at the floating creature for a moment, then regained his composure. "Toll? I—Wait a minute! What do you mean, the Olympians cheated?"

"Not important!" Charon growled. His face flashed briefly to a wounded expression. "What matters now is they're permanent residents of the Underworld, trapped in the prison Tartarus."

"Tartarus?" Zeus's brow furrowed. "Seems like a silly place to hunt for Hades's magic cap. Mind pointing me that way so I can go bust them out?"

"You want to join your little gang of cheating misfits do you, Zeus?" Charon asked. "Pay me one obol, and I shall ferry you across."

Zeus raised his eyebrows. "So you Underworld types know me, huh?" He puffed up a little with pride. "I mean, of course you do: I'm me."

Charon was unamused. "Pay me or leave."

Zeus patted the sides of his robes. "Huh, must have left my obols in my other chiton." Zeus turned and pointed upstream. "Oh, look! Is that a Hydra?!"

Charon turned to look.

Zeus scurried out onto Poseidon's lifeline, stretching his arms for balance as he crossed it like a tightrope above the dark currents. He was halfway across the river when Charon caught on.

"Cheater!" the creature called. He slammed his body into the lifeline, making it twang like a guitar string.

"Whoa!" Zeus had no choice but to leap off his wobbling tightrope. He splashed gracelessly into the knee-deep water and scrambled up the riverbank at full sprint, still following Poseidon's lifeline.

"That's right, you keep going, cheater!" Charon screamed after him. "You can go straight to Hades!"

CHAPTER 33

"**YOU OKAY DOWN THERE, BUDDY?**"
Hermes, along with Athena and Demeter, stood at the edge of Ares's hole. The pug had uncovered a metal grate clogged with wet sand, and his front legs had fallen between its bars.

"I'm fine, I'm fine," Ares said, finding his footing again atop the grate. Eager to keep digging, he used his paws to clear the sand between the bars of the grate. The wet clumps fell into the darkness below, landing with a soft splash.

With the grate cleared, they could all see that a river flowed below, slow-moving and shallow. "That might be our way out," Demeter said. "You see any way to open that grate, Ares?"

"I think I do!" Hermes squawked. She hopped down to join Ares and eyeballed the grate beneath their feet. "I guess this prison has bars after all." She stomped on the cold metal. "But in our case, they might be our ticket out of here." She turned to Ares. "Let me see Hippolyta's belt, buddy."

The pug tilted his head at her. "You don't think Hades is watching, do you?" he asked Hermes.

She reached up and gently unhooked the chain. "If he is, then this is his last chance to stop us from escaping this prison. You're going to get us out of here!" The hen looped the chain from Ares's collar down through the bars of the grate.

"I need you to back up, buddy!" Hermes said to Ares. "Pull!"

"Nnnngg." The pug grunted as he strained to open the grate. The chain grew taut against Ares's collar, which dug into the back of his neck. Ares grimaced but didn't give up. Suddenly, the grate rose slightly.

"You're doing it!" Demeter rooted him on. Not for the first time she was wowed by the war god's strength.

"Nnnnng!" Ares legs began sinking into the wet

sand. He was losing traction. The grate sunk back into the stone floor.

"Lemme lend a wing!" Hermes hopped behind him and tugged at his shoulder.

Athena padded down beside Hermes. "Grab on!" Hermes wrapped her other wing around Athena's torso, and the cat added her strength to the struggle. All three found their footing, and the grate began to rise again.

"One more big pull and you'll have it!" Demeter

coached from above. "On three! One, two—"

SHOOMP! The grate suddenly fell open, sending Ares, Hermes, and Athena tumbling backward into each other.

Demeter whooped. "We have an exit!"

Athena ran to the open hole. It was a short drop to the shallow river below. She eyed the water unhappily. "Someone want to go first? Anyone?"

"I'll go!" Demeter hopped into the water with a shallow splash.

Hermes scrambled to unhook the chain from the grate. When she moved to hook it just around his collar again, Ares held up a paw. "You can have Hippolyta's belt back. I don't need it anymore."

"Ya never did, pal." Hermes clapped her friend on the shoulder and wrapped the chain around her chest, then jumped into the hole. Ares followed.

Athena sighed and dropped last. The shallow water barely covered her paws, but it was extra mucky from all the sand Ares had sent into it. Athena saw that the river ran through a narrow tunnel lit faintly by the now-familiar green moss. They only had two directions to choose from: upstream or downstream.

"I wonder what river this is," said Athena. "Ares, take a taste and let us know how you feel."

"Okay!" The pug took a few paces upstream to get to clearer water and lapped up a few tonguefuls. "Ach." He made a sour face, and his eyes turned yellow.

"It's the Acheron!" Demeter exclaimed.

"I suspected as much," Athena said. "Decision time, Olympians: We can either head downstream and find our way back to Greece, or go upstream for one more crack at that cap."

"The Oracle said only those 'nimble, cunning, resilient, and strong enough' could reach Hades's throne room," Demeter reminded them. "We definitely have the right stuff."

"We've risen to every challenge down here," Hermes agreed. "Why stop now?"

Ares, his eyes already back to normal, didn't hesitate. He bolted upstream without another word. Before his curly tail faded into the distance, the other Olympians headed after him.

CHAPTER 34

EUS'S LEGS ACHED. HIS LUNGS BURNED. HE
had been following Poseidon's lifeline for what
seemed like too long. "Artie ... was right,"
he muttered. "I wish I hadn't left Mount Olympus."

Finally, he came to a pool of dark water fed by a
pounding waterfall into which Poseidon's lifeline
vanished. Zeus scoured the banks of the pool for where
the lifeline exited and continued on. It didn't!

He tugged at the line, but it wouldn't budge. Zeus
scanned the shore for clues as to where to go to next.
Nothing.

Frustrated, he yelled, "Poseidon, are you down
there?!"

"Nope, he's busy carrying the weight of the world!"

Zeus was shocked to get a reply. The voice sounded strangely familiar. He leaned over and stared into the dark water. "Ares? That you?"

"Yep! That's me!" came Ares's voice, so close that Zeus nearly toppled into the pool. He watched in amazement as the war god emerged from behind the waterfall, followed by Athena, Demeter, and Hermes.

"Zeus!" Athena exclaimed.

"What are you doing here?!" Demeter asked.

"I gave that three-headed mighty mutt the slip so I could bust you out of uncharted territory," Zeus said, proudly crossing his arms. The Olympians stared at him. "Don't everyone applaud at once."

"We already escaped Tartarus," Demeter said, shrugging.

"Not all of you," Zeus said, looking again at Poseidon's lifeline where it entered the dark water. "Where's the sea lord?"

"He's still in there." Ares waved a paw toward the waterfall. Zeus walked around the pool and discovered the slippery path behind it leading to a grotto. A large grate lay open on the floor, water pouring into it.

"That's how we got out of Tartarus," Athena explained. "The River Acheron was the only way out of that miserable hole."

Zeus spotted Poseidon's lifeline stretching toward a cave entrance behind the waterfall. "Poseidon's in there?"

"Yep," Hermes replied. "He's in the House of Hades holdin' up the world."

"The House of Hades?!" Zeus did a double take. "Did you find the Cap?"

Demeter shuffled her legs. "Not quite," she admitted. "We know where it is, though."

"You found Hades's throne room?"

Athena nodded toward the cave entrance. "I left a trail."

"Okay, good work." Zeus nodded approvingly. "You managed to accomplish a lot without me."

"We took turns leading," Hermes said proudly.

"And each time we took a vote," Demeter added.

"It was a dogocracy," Ares said solemnly.

"Democracy," Athena corrected.

"Democracy, huh?" Zeus repeated, shaking his head. "Well, there'll be no more of that now that I'm back."

"Oh, really?" Demeter replied. "So you have a plan worked out to get into the throne room, nab the Cap, free Poseidon, then get back to Greece, all before sunrise?" She crossed her four front legs and stared at Zeus.

"Sure I do," he answered, although he was shuffling his feet and staring at the ground, unwilling to meet the Olympians' eyes. Finally he looked up. "But I'm open to suggestions?"

"I suggest we call in some help from our friends," Demeter chimed in at once.

Zeus tilted his head. "What friends?"

"Persephone and the Underworldlings!"

"Persef-a-who?" Zeus stumbled over the name.

"She's Demeter's biggest fan," Ares explained.

"It's a Bugcropolis thing," Demeter added.
"Persephone leads the denizens of the Underworld,
dozens of them. They all got lulled to sleep by this
smooth-talking snake named Hypnos. But Hermes is
immune to Hypnos's powers. She can reverse his spell."

"That so?" Zeus eyed Hermes.

"Goddess of sleep," the hen said, jabbing a wing at
her chest. "I'm good at more than just delivering
messages, you know."

"These Underworldlings," Zeus said, "they have no
loyalty to Hades?"

"None at all," Demeter assured him. "They think he's
a big bully. He scared them with his thunder and then
trapped them down here."

"His thunder, huh? Might be time to teach these
Underworldlings a thing or two about Hades." Zeus
rubbed his chin thoughtfully and turned to Demeter
and Hermes. "Gang, we need to split up one more time."

CHAPTER 35

ZEUS THE MIGHTY STOOD AT THE ENTRANCE to Hades's throne room and smoothed his royal chiton. He had been waiting for this moment since Hades's magic tricks and phony thunder had chased him out of the Underworld at their previous meeting. Zeus couldn't wait to show Hades who was boss. He stepped into the round, cavernous room, followed by Ares and Athena. Demeter and Hermes weren't with them.

Even by Underworld standards, the throne room was a wild place, crisscrossed with what must have been every pipe in the land. The pipes met in the center of the ceiling, where they extended downward and formed Hades's throne, which sat empty on a rock-strewn island in the center of the room. A simple stone bridge crossed the moat, the only connection between the island and the rest of the room. Guarding the throne were a large tortoise and a coiled snake, with indigo scales. The Cap of Shadows was nowhere to be seen.

"Hypnos and Atlas, I presume." Zeus spoke to the tortoise first.

"I'm Atlas. He's—"

"Don't care," Zeus said, cutting Atlas off. "Just here to see your boss."

Hypnos said nothing, but his head began bobbing left and right while his eyes strobed from silver to gold to indigo.

"No, no, no, we're not doing this again." Athena waved her paws at Zeus and Ares. "Ignore the snake. Pretend he's not here. We don't need a nap."

Zeus focused on Atlas. "Tell Hades to get his sneaky butt on in here. He's got something I want."

"Tell him yourself," Atlas snapped, gesturing toward the empty throne, which was about Zeus's size. "He's right there."

Zeus, Athena, and Ares eyed the throne. Its seat and

back were made of ornate metal discs, but they saw nothing in it. Before they could question Atlas, Hades's voice boomed, "YOU SHALL PAY DEARLY FOR ENTERING MY SANCTUM UNBIDDEN!"

Zeus pretended to shiver with fright. "Ooh, what are you going to do? Try to scare me with your phony thunder tricks?"

KRAKOW!! Thunder clapped right above the Olympians' heads. Ares flinched but held his ground, no longer needing his thunder-repelling chain.

Zeus raised a finger and tilted his ear toward the pipes crisscrossing the ceiling. "That thunder— something about it isn't right."

"SILENCE!" Hades boomed. The room grew quiet.

Which allowed the Olympians to hear Hermes's song in the distance.

CHAPTER 36

ATHENA LEANED FORWARD NEXT TO ZEUS and pretended to preen a paw. "Reinforcements are on the way," she whispered. Zeus folded his paws behind his back and gave Athena a thumbs-up. He only needed to keep Hades distracted for a few more minutes.

"What's the thumbs-up for, boss?" Ares shouted gleefully.

"Shush," Athena hissed at him.

"So, Hades, I take it you're wearing your Cap of Shadows?" Zeus casually strolled across the stone bridge onto the island.

Hades waited a long moment before answering, "OBVIOUSLY."

"Aren't you worried about someone walking off with it?" Zeus continued, inching closer. "I mean, without your three-headed guard mutt here to protect it?"

"HUMPH," Hades scoffed. "IMPOSSIBLE."

"Cerberus was supposed to keep me locked in my palace." Zeus stepped carefully around the rocks on the island. "Yet here I am. You might want to reconsider what you think is impossible."

KRAKKKKOWWW!! Another mighty thunderclap erupted. "There it is again—that weird *gonk* sound," Zeus said. He looked up in time to see one of the pipes clang against the rocky ceiling.

Zeus grinned. He had Hades right where he wanted him. Almost. "Just curious, Hades," Zeus kept chatting as he crept forward, paws behind his back. "Do you have to take off your clothes after you put on the Cap? Otherwise, we'd see your robes or whatever floating around like a ghost?"

"OF COURSE NOT," Hades answered impatiently.

"Huh, is that right?" Zeus whistled. "Well, that's a neat trick." He was less than a foot from Hades's throne now. "What would happen if you ate something while you're invisible? Would it turn invisible when you swallowed it, or would we see all the gross chewed-up bits going down your gullet?"

"WHY DO YOU INSIST ON MOCKING ME?"

A rumbling sound came from just outside the throne room.

"Two reasons, actually." Zeus held up two fingers. "One, because I'm really good at it. And two, because I'm trying to distract you."

CHAPTER 37

SUDDENLY, A SPOTTED GUINEA PIG CHARGED
into the throne room. He was followed by
moles and voles, burrowing owls and gophers,
chipmunks and skunks—all digging animals, dozens
of them. They stampeded into the cavernous chamber,
filling the space around the moat. When Hermes
and Demeter entered behind everyone else, along
with a mole cricket, Zeus gave them a grateful bow.
"Persephone, isn't it?" he asked the cricket.

"I know you!" she trilled. "You're Zeus, one of
Demeter's Olympians!"

Zeus's white patch twitched. "One of *Demeter's*
Olympians?"

"WHAT IS THE MEANING OF THIS?!" the lord of

the Underworld boomed. "THESE ANIMALS ARE FORBIDDEN FROM ENTERING MY HOUSE!"

"That's a rotten way to treat your subjects," Zeus said. He was mere inches from Hades's throne.

Hypnos slithered forward, furious. "How dare you awaken the Underworldlings!"

"I think they've slept long enough." Zeus gestured to the surrounding animals. "Allow me to open their eyes to the truth!" In one swift motion, he plopped onto the throne. As he'd suspected, it was empty. Zeus turned and spun the metal disc that formed the throne's back.

KRAKOWWWW! The pipes gonked into the ceiling, providing the thunder Zeus expected. "See that, Underworldlings? Hades's thunder is just a trick."

The Underworldlings gasped. "Hades is a phony?" Persephone yelled. The animals around her started chanting, "Phony! Phony! Phony!" in a strange, low tone that the Olympians could barely hear. Soon the chant echoed off the vaulted ceiling.

"SILENCE!" Hades screamed, but the chanting continued.

Finally, one of the bigger rocks nearby lifted off the ground and hovered in place for a moment before zooming toward Zeus's head. The Underworldlings' chanting ceased, replaced with fearful gasps.

"About time we meet face to face, Hades!" Zeus stood up. When the rock reached him, he ducked and grabbed at what appeared to be empty air behind it. His paws connected with something cold and hard.

Zeus came away holding a red bucket-shaped cap. A black mole wearing a red cape materialized with a squeak beneath it. He clutched the rock that had been heading for Zeus.

The Underworldlings gawked. A few giggled.

"You know, Hades," Zeus said. "I figured you wouldn't look so tough without your magic hat, and boy was I ever right."

The mole was Zeus's size, with itty-bitty pinprick eyes and a pink snout. In his paws, he clutched the rock inches from Zeus's face.

Without answering, the mole dropped his rock on Zeus's toe.

"Ow!" Zeus clutched his foot, letting the red cap fall to the floor. Hades let out an excited squeak, grabbed the cap, and tucked it under his arm as he dashed toward his throne, his cape billowing behind him. Fearful that Hades was about to turn invisible again, Zeus latched on to the hem of the cape.

"Give it up, Hades," he said, tugging the cape with both paws. "You can't get away."

But Hades remained hidden behind his throne. Hypnos and Atlas, still on either side of it, seemed to be looking for an escape route. Worried about what the lord of the Underworld was up to, Zeus took two steps closer. "No use hiding, Ha—"

The mole suddenly popped into view, his cape askew on its golden chain from Zeus's tugging. He held out the Cap of Shadows. "You wish to borrow my magic cap?" The mole's voice was a mere squeak when it wasn't amplified by the bucket-like cap. "Very well, then. You win. Congratulations." He tossed it to Zeus, who caught it clumsily and then raised the Cap to his head.

"Now just go, will you? You've certainly caused me enough grief." Hades waved at the army of angry Underworldlings.

Zeus tucked the Cap beneath his arm and hurried toward the surprised Olympians. "Sure, sure," he agreed, barely able to hide his glee. "You do have your paws full. It seems like your subjects woke up on the wrong side of the bed."

"I … I can't believe Hades just gave you his most precious treasure," Athena said.

"Smartest thing he could've done. He knew he'd met his match. C'mon, we should really be getting home."

The mob of animals parted for Zeus and his team as they left the throne room. Zeus stopped when he reached Persephone. "Thanks for rallying the troops."

"Don't thank me! Thank her!" She looked at Demeter in reverence. "She's the one that sent your hen friend to wake everyone up."

Demeter beamed, then shrugged. "Technically it's true."

Zeus glanced back. Hades was already nowhere to be seen, and Atlas and Hypnos hadn't budged. "I don't think these guys'll give you any more trouble," he told Persephone. Then, addressing all of the animals, he announced, "The Underworld is all yours now."

"Uh, no thanks," Persephone replied. "We've spent enough time down here in the dark."

"Oh, good," Demeter said, "because I think we need your Underworldlings' special talents to get home. Won't you follow us?"

Zeus tilted his head at Demeter's words but led the way out of the throne room. The Olympians fell into line, and behind them marched the Underworldlings, a parade of burrowing animals.

Thanks to the paw prints Athena had left at each portal, they quickly navigated the maze of rooms in the House of Hades. It wasn't long before they came to the cavern where Poseidon still held up the roof of the world.

"Zeus!" Poseidon exclaimed. "Please tell me you've acquired the Cap."

"You mean this?" Zeus held it up. "Mission accomplished! I did it!"

"Ahem, *we* did it," Demeter corrected. "I mean, we all took turns leading."

"Yeah, we're a dogocracy," Ares agreed.

"How about we chalk it up to good ol' Olympian mojo?" Hermes suggested.

Poseidon's eyes widened as the Underworldlings filed in. "I see you woke Demeter's fan club."

"It's a good thing we did." Demeter turned to Persephone. "Do you think the burrowers among you could relieve our friend Poseidon here of his burden?"

Persephone nodded and waved over a brown shrew. The two consulted in low tones. The Olympians watched nervously as the shrew gestured to the floor and ceiling. Zeus's white cheek patch twitched.

Finally, Persephone stepped forward "Good news!" she announced. "My friend here believes we're in a sinkhole."

"Yay!" Ares cheered, then stopped short. "What's a sinkhole?"

"I can't believe I'm saying this," Athena chimed in, "but Ares has a good question."

"Sinkholes are enchanted spots where the borders between the Underworld and the sunlit realm are thin," Persephone explained. The Olympians blinked at her. "The exit is right up there!" She pointed a stubby leg toward the ceiling Poseidon held up.

"And you Underworldlings can open this exit?" Hermes asked.

"Definitely," Persephone assured them, "but you might want to duck." Before anyone could ask why, Persephone turned to the burrowing animals around her. "Let's blow the roof off this joint!"

With a wild cheer, a pack of Underworldlings raced up the mound, surrounding Poseidon. They climbed atop each other, clambering to dig out the ceiling. Claylike chunks began breaking into smaller pieces and rained down on the startled Olympians. It wasn't long before the whole thing collapsed.

CHAPTER 38

"**W**HAT JUST HAPPENED?" ZEUS STOOD blinking in the fresh orange light bathing all of them.

"Persephone was right!" Demeter leapt up a stack of debris and peered over the top of the pit. "Olympians, the sinkhole really is an exit!! To the northern lands!"

It took a moment for them to realize they were covered in only a thin layer of dust and rubble. Most of the Underworldlings were already wandering out to enjoy their freedom. Only Persephone lingered. Behind her, Zeus took in all the northern lands spots that he knew: the enchanted apple tree, Ares's obstacle course, and, most important, the dog-size portal back to Greece. The area was soaked from the rainstorm of the night before, although the skies were clear now. But Zeus realized with alarm that the warm orange light was coming from the rising sun.

"Time to get home!" Zeus ran toward the portal with Hades's cap tucked under an arm. Demeter turned to follow him, but paused and then leapt over to Persephone. "You coming with us?" she asked the mole cricket. "I'm sure you can go back home to the Bugcropolis."

Persephone looked longingly toward the portal, then shook her head. "No, I think I'll stick to my original plan. I'm going to tour the world like my hero, Demeter." She smiled.

"Demeter, hurry up!" Zeus called. The other Olympians were already filing back through the portal to Greece.

"Coming!" Demeter shouted. She turned back to say farewell to Persephone, but the mole cricket was gone.

Within moments, they were back in Greece. "Hold up," Zeus ordered, waving everyone into the shadow of Mount Olympus. "I'll make sure the path is clear." To the east, the Aegean Sea glittered in the morning sunlight. To the west, the *Argo* stood where Zeus had left it, wedged in the open portal to uncharted territory. Athena's stick toy still stood on its stern.

All was quiet.

"Well, Artie and Callie aren't here yet, thank the gods!" Zeus said.

"Mutt Nuggets, here I come!" Ares started to bolt, but Zeus leapt in front of him.

"Stay, boy!" he commanded. "Cerberus is still keeping watch!"

"Right, Cerberus!" Demeter clapped four legs. "He'll see all of you once we leave the shadow of Mount Olympus."

"How'd you get past him anyway, Zeus?" Hermes asked.

"Zeus Deuce!" he exclaimed.

When he saw the Olympians' confused expressions, he added, "Long story. I'll go take care of Cerberus now." Zeus hefted Hades's Cap. "Time to put this thing to use."

"I think we have bigger problems than Cerberus." Athena's eyes had locked on the main portal to Greece. The Olympians heard the rattling of keys. Artie stepped through the door, followed by Callie.

"Good morning, everybody!" Artie called. "Did you miss us?"

CHAPTER 39

ARTIE BEGAN SWITCHING ON LIGHTS while Callie walked toward the rear of the shop. So far they hadn't noticed the Olympians clustered near the back door.

"We could all use a Cap of Shadows right about now," Athena whispered. "What do we do?"

"Quit worrying," said Zeus, full of confidence. "I'm in charge again! I'll distract Artie and Callie, and then deal with that three-headed hound up there." He jabbed a thumb toward Cerberus. "Everyone sneak home!"

Before anyone could respond, Zeus slipped on the Cap, which came down to his chin. He spun it around to line his eyes up with the Cap's tiny eyeholes, then took off at a run.

After a moment, Hermes asked, "Y'all can still see him, right? Or is it just me?"

"It's not just you," Athena replied nervously. Zeus was headed directly toward Callie. "Maybe the Cap only works in the Underworld? Or … do you think Hades might've pulled a switcheroo?" She wanted to call out to Zeus, but he was already too far away and in plain sight of Callie, who had turned toward their corner of Greece.

"Hey!" Callie exclaimed. "How'd my robot vacuum get stuck in the door to—"

"Woof! Woof! Woof!" Cerberus barked up on Mount Olympus. Flashing eyes locked on Zeus. If anything, Hades's invisibility cap made him even more visible, its vibrant red calling attention to the hamster.

Callie stood dumbstruck as the hamster put on his strange little show. He barreled through a display of scratching posts, making them wobble. He picked up a crumb of Mutt Nuggets and ran back and forth with it in front of Callie. "WOOOO!" He was making a small sort of moaning noise, his voice amplified by the Cap. "WOOOO!"

"Um, Artie?" she said. "You really need to come see this."

"Now what?" replied Artie, who was about to scrub the walls of the aquarium. She set down her brush and walked over to Callie. Together, the two women watched Zeus scurrying around, picking up and dropping various toys and treats.

Zeus was in the middle of dragging a ball chucker across the floor when he saw the Olympians still assembled and staring at him. "WHAT ARE YOU WAITING FOR? GO HOME!" he yelled. "THEY TOTALLY THINK I'M A GHOST!"

"Why does he think they think he's a ghost?" Ares asked. "If I can see Zeus, they can see him, right?"

"He's busted," Demeter replied flatly. "The Cap's a crock."

"That doesn't matter now," Athena hissed. "Zeus is busted, but he's also right. This is our chance! Everyone get home!" The Olympians silently headed for their respective living quarters. After zipping up the rope behind Mount Olympus and squeezing into the palace, Demeter made sure each of her fellow Olympians was safe. Thanks to Hades's malfunctioning cap, Cerberus kept all three of his heads focused solely on Zeus.

Zeus had counted a few beats to allow the Olympians enough time to scramble home. Now he made a beeline for Mount Olympus, where he scurried up the hidden rope to his palace.

"Where's Zeus going now?" Artie whispered. She went to grab the hamster, but Callie put a hand on her arm.

"Wait, wait, please. I gotta see what he does next." Instead of entering his palace, Zeus dashed to its eastern edge and threw his weight against Cerberus's doghouse. It took two great heaves, but he succeeded in knocking it off the mountaintop. "BAD DOG!" Zeus hollered as the hut tumbled to the ground far below.

"I didn't see *that* coming," Callie said.

"Zeus! We can see you! Everyone can see you!" Demeter called.

But her words didn't register. Zeus was too busy celebrating his defeat of Cerberus. Finally he leapt triumphantly into his palace. "AND ... HOME! Did you see their faces when they saw that floating Mutt Nugget?" He whooped and tossed a piece of Fuzzy Feast into the air. "I didn't look. I was too busy putting on the performance of a lifetime!"

He turned toward Demeter and noticed she was watching his every move. "Wait, what did you just say?"

"Everyone can see you. I can see you right now."

"Impossible!" Zeus scoffed. "How?"

"With my eyes," Demeter answered.

"I repeat, impossible!" Zeus said. He yanked off the Cap and examined it. "It worked when Hades wore it." His white patch quivered. "You don't think ... ? Could he have swapped caps on me? When he was hiding behind his throne? What—"

A clapping sound interrupted Zeus. He turned toward Greece to find Artie and Callie smiling and applauding him.

"That sure was quite the show you put on for us, Zeus," Callie said.

"And now I know how my little escape artist is getting out every night," Artie replied. "Well, we can put an end to that!" She reached behind Zeus's habitat and yanked off the string he had used to climb home. Then she took a stiff piece of twine and tied the door's opening shut.

Zeus was once again a prisoner in his own palace.

CHAPTER 40

I DON'T UNDERSTAND." ZEUS WAS STILL
sitting, stunned, staring at Hades's cap where
he had tossed it in the corner of his palace.
"Why could everyone see me?"

"BECAUSE YOU'RE A FOOL," replied a familiar
booming voice. It sounded like it came from just outside
Zeus's palace.

Hades materialized at the locked back entrance.
Above his head he held a glimmering red cap—the real
Cap of Shadows.

"What ... what do you mean?" Zeus stammered.

"Do you really believe I would give you my most
powerful artifact?" the mole squeaked, regarding them
with beady eyes. "Why do you think I let your silly

Olympians escape from Tartarus?"

"Let us escape?" Demeter repeated. She looked at Zeus. "What's he going on about?"

"You took the bait, Zeus!" Hades gloated. "I figured the phony cap would eventually get you into trouble and keep you out of my realm for good, but I never dreamed it would happen so fast!" He pulled at the twine Artie had fastened to the palace. "More secure than Tartarus. Ha!" With that, Hades put the real Cap back on his head—and blinked out of sight.

"Wait! Hades!" Zeus shouted at the empty spot where the mole had been. "What's the rush?! How about helping a fellow god out? We could strike a deal! You unlock my back door and I'll … I'll …" He couldn't finish the thought.

"You'll what?" Hades had pulled off his invisibility cap and materialized once more.

"I'll let you rule the Underworld in peace!" Zeus offered.

Hades smirked. "Already doing that."

"I'll vow not to seek furious revenge!" Zeus tried.

Hades shrugged. "I'll take my chances."

"I'll—I'll—" Zeus sputtered as he cast around for ideas. "I'll give this back!" He held up the red cap he'd mistaken for the real one.

Now Hades chuckled. "Keep it," he said. "Souvenir." He slipped the Cap of Shadows on again and vanished.

Zeus walked toward the pillars of his palace, his shoulders slumped. He gazed out over Greece and found Artie and Callie inspecting Cerberus at the foot of Mount Olympus.

"I can't get it to upload last night's videos." Artie held Cerberus upside down in her hands. "It's pretty banged up."

"Lemme see what I can do with it." Callie took Cerberus, and the two women walked away.

Zeus sunk miserably to the floor. Demeter hopped cautiously to his side but had no idea how to console him.

"Artie was right," he finally said.

"About what?" Demeter asked.

"She said one of these days I'd wish I'd never left my palace."

"Don't worry, pal!" Demeter tried to sound cheerful. "You'll figure a way out of this! You always do!"

Without answering, Zeus made his way to his exercise wheel—where he nearly tripped over a length of rope that stretched from the wheel to the edge of the palace.

"What's this—" Zeus's face lit up. "Zeus Deuce!"

He ran to the pillars and peered straight down. His clone was still lying where it had landed at the foot of Mount Olympus, somehow unnoticed by Artie and

Callie. Zeus tugged at the rope, and Zeus Deuce twitched.

Demeter stepped to Zeus's side and squinted down the mountain. "What in the world is that thing?"

"That," Zeus replied happily, "might just be my way out." He hopped in his exercise wheel and began sprinting, winding the rope and winching up the clone he'd made from the Nemean cloak.

Demeter watched the ratty dummy rise toward the palace. "I don't understand," she said.

"Maybe what I need right now isn't invisibility but *invincibility*," Zeus the Mighty explained, barely winded despite his sprinting. "That cloak helped us defeat the Hydra. I'm sure I can use it to bust out of my own palace."

THE TRUTH BEHIND THE FICTION

Myths on the Map

Ancient Greece was both a time and a place: a civilization that flourished near the Aegean and Mediterranean Seas around 2,500 years ago. It was a realm of heroic mortals ruled by fearsome gods who didn't always get along. Or so Greek mythology would have us believe. How seriously should we take these myths? Are they history lessons or fairy tales? Actually, they're a bit of both.

What Is a Myth?

A myth is a special kind of story that tries to explain something. Myths helped people make sense of their world in the days before science and internet search engines. Why does the sun set? Why does the earth shake? Where did the world come from? Myths offered supernatural solutions to these mysteries by explaining that a gaggle of gods and goddesses controlled them. Ancient Greeks took these stories for fact, building temples and holding lavish events to appease

Olympian gods had their own colossal temples. This one was built for Zeus in Athens and once had more than a hundred columns.

196

the gods. The original Olympic Games were actually
created in honor of Zeus.

The Mythmakers

No one knows who first came up with the Greek
myths. The tales weren't written until around 800 B.C.,
when a poet named Homer composed his two epic
poems, *The Iliad* and *The Odyssey*. The stories were
an account of a conflict called the Trojan War and
featured Greek gods and mortal humans. Homer
didn't bother explaining who his characters were because ancient
Greeks already knew all about them from their own songs and poems.

To Be Continued ...

Even after the civilization of ancient Greece fell under Roman rule
more than 2,000 years ago, Greek culture lived on and its myths were
not forgotten. The Romans simply adapted them for their own use.
Modern-day authors, playwrights, and screenwriters do the same
thing, tweaking and retelling myths for
audiences.

Today, Greek mythology's influence
can be found everywhere, from
movies to store names and
clothing brands. The Greeks' myths
established the "hero's journey"—a
formula featured in stories ranging
from Star Wars to Harry Potter: a hero
yearning for adventure, a series of
dangerous trials, help or hindrance
from the supernatural, and victory
over impossible odds. Sound familiar?

**Athena marches in the
middle of a parade of gods
on this ancient Greek vase.**

The ancient Greeks worshipped 12 major gods known as the Olympians (because they gathered on Mount Olympus, the highest peak on Earth). These gods were all-powerful, and yet they possessed the same emotions—love, sadness, anger, jealousy—as everyday mortals.

Zeus

King of the gods, Zeus ruled from Mount Olympus and held domain over the heavens and the land beneath them. He brought order, making sure none of the Olympians got out of line.

Poseidon

God of all bodies of water, Poseidon commanded the tides using his enchanted trident. Sailors prayed to him for safe passage. He was a brother to Zeus. Like some siblings, they didn't always get along.

Hades

Another brother of Zeus, Hades chose the mysterious realm of the Underworld for his kingdom. There he sat on his bronze throne and ruled over an odd assortment of monsters and mortals. They were welcome to enter his land of the dead, but they could never leave.

Athena

Goddess of wisdom, Athena was the brains of the Olympian operation. She also inspired creativity. When ancient Greeks wanted to build something, they prayed to Athena for inspiration.

Ares

Few Greek gods were as feared as Ares, the god of war. He was a brute, a force of chaos. He attacked first and asked questions ... never! Warriors screamed his name before charging into battle.

Demeter

As the goddess of food and the harvest, Demeter was beloved by ancient Greeks. One bad season of crops could lead to disaster. Demeter kept everyone's belly full.

Artemis

A guardian and caretaker, Artemis was the goddess of animals, protecting the young and helpless. She lived in the wilderness, tending to her furry and feathered friends.

Hermes

With his feathered sandals and winged hat, Hermes was the most graceful of the Olympian gods, which is one reason they chose him as their messenger. Mortals prayed to him when they needed wit, trickery, or even a good night's sleep.

AMAZING ARTIFACTS

Greek mythology is rich with relics enchanted with astounding powers.

Nemean Cloak

The ancient Greek region of Nemea was the home to a monster lion whose hide was impervious to weapons. Heracles the hero was charged with subduing it and saving the locals. He wrestled it into submission and wore its hide as a trophy. The hide made Heracles equally indestructible.

Cap of Invisibility

A powerful relic on par with Poseidon's trident, this simple cap granted its wearer the ability to blend into the scenery and hide in plain sight. It was forged by a cyclops blacksmith and gifted to Hades. He guarded it with all the power of the Underworld.

The Myth of Hades and the Underworld

The Underworld was a mysterious and dark realm of stark mountain ranges, ghostly fields, bottomless lakes, and black rivers. The poet Homer wrote that the Underworld was located on the far western edge of the world, yet, if one knew where to look, it could be accessed by secret portals, often in caves or in the lightless depths of lakes.

Enter If You Dare

The Underworld was crisscrossed by five rivers, each tied to a different emotion or ill effect. Those who drank from the River Lethe fell into a trancelike state, while the muddy waters of the River Acheron brought misery and a sour stomach. The Underworld's entrance was marked by the River Styx, a frigid river that caused rage. Only the boatman Charon (pronounced Kah-run) could ferry visitors across—but the ride wasn't free.

Hades's Home, Sweet Home

Dark and cold, creepy and vast, the Underworld chilled the blood of mortals. But to the god Hades, it was a paradise. Hades was a brother of Zeus and Poseidon. While Poseidon claimed all water as

his domain and Zeus ruled over the land, Hades had his eye on the dark spaces beneath. He liked the Underworld's perpetual darkness, its odd and grotesque residents. It came with its own prison, called Tartarus, a bottomless abyss where Hades might keep his enemies. He created a sprawling mansion, the House of Hades, in which he sat on a bronze throne. From there he ruled his realm as a home for the dead. Hades welcomed the deceased under one condition: They were never allowed to leave.

The toll to enter the Underworld was two coins—called obols. In some parts of ancient Greece, people were buried with a coin on each eye so they would have the correct change for the ferryman Charon.

Meet the Underworldlings

Aside from Charon, Hades's boatman, the Underworld was home to Hypnos, the master of sleep. Here also was Atlas, who was doomed to carry the weight of the heavens on his shoulders. Cronos (the evil father of Zeus, Poseidon, and Hades) was sentenced to eternity in Tartarus. Craving friendlier company, Hades lured Persephone, the daughter of Demeter, to his realm. But Demeter wanted Persephone returned and choked off all harvests and threatened to plunge the world into starvation until Zeus sent Hermes the winged god to retrieve her. Perhaps the most famous resident of the Underworld was Cerberus. Hades sent his watchdog to patrol the borders of his realm. Nothing got past the fearsome fangs of this dog's three heads!

Escape Artistry

Although it was meant to be a place of no return, mortals did find their way in and out of the Underworld. Theseus, slayer of the Minotaur, visited briefly. So did the hero Heracles. One of the 12 labors he was charged with was retrieving Cerberus the guard dog. Heracles completed this challenge by battling past Charon and dragging the three-headed hound from the Underworld by his collar. Hades was powerless to stop the mighty mortal—proving that the Underworld wasn't so escape-proof after all.

Athens, Georgia, United States

Athens, Greece

Athens, Georgia, is about 5,600 miles (9,000 km) away from Athens, Greece.

SERBIA

KOSOVO

NORTH MACEDONIA

ALBANIA

Mount Olympus

ITALY

ADRIATIC SEA

GREECE

River Acheron

TYRRHENIAN SEA

IONIAN SEA

Delphi

This scenic river carves through gorges and into caverns, where ancient Greeks believed it flowed into the Underworld as a black river of misery.

Corinth

Nemea

Argos

Strait of Messina

SICILY

Sparta

Taenarum

At the height of its power around 800 B.C., ancient Greece was a sprawling empire. While its geography divided it into many separate regions, they all shared the same language, culture, and—most important—mythology.

MAP KEY

◆ Ancient location

● Ancient city

■ Area controlled by Greece around 500 B.C.

— Present-day boundary

The poet Homer wrote that the entrance to the Underworld was at the far western edge of the world, although Heracles found a secret entrance in a cavern near the ancient town of Taenarum.

To Colchis

BULGARIA

BLACK SEA

The highest peak in ancient Greece, Mount Olympus was home to Zeus and was where he held court over the Olympians.

T U R K E Y

Sea of Marmara

Troy

AEGEAN SEA

Thebes

Athens

Miletus

Sea of Crete

C R E T E

Knossos

0 — 100 miles

0 — 100 kilometers

M E D I T E R R A N E A N   S E A

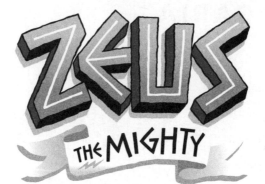

BOOK 5

The Voyage on the Oddest Sea

THE OLYMPIANS GATHERED AT THE WATER'S edge, next to Zeus's newly assembled boat. He was busy stowing sacks of Fuzzy Feast and extra lettuce bits for their voyage on the Oddest Sea. The boat's shiny hull glowed a deep crimson in the red light cast by the Mount Olympus Pet Center sign. The disc-shaped sail was lowered face down on its rubber-bone mast, ready for hoisting. Zeus's replica, Zeus Deuce, was strapped upright at the bow of the bowl.

Hermes looked over the finished product and whistled. "For such a mangy ball of fluff, ol' Zeus Deuce makes a pretty good figurehead."

"The best figurehead," Zeus said absentmindedly as he swept the last few crumbs of Ares's Mutt Nuggets from the bottom of the boat, then buffed out a spot of slobber on the hull.

Beside the boat, Athena and Ares finished leaning two long orange plastic tubes against the steep shoreline of the Aegean Sea. The tubes would serve as a ramp to launch the boat into the water. A string ran to a metal loop at the top of the tubes and back to Zeus's boat.

Hermes positioned the boat at the bottom of the ramp. Zeus and Demeter hopped aboard and arranged the lines they would use to raise sail.

Meanwhile, Athena paced nervously along the shoreline. "I really advise you to put this adventure off for just a night or two," she said, "until I can adapt the *Argo* and we can all go."

Zeus's cheek patch quivered. He looked ready to argue, but his expression softened. "Look, I appreciate you lookin' out for me," he said. "But remember: I'm the king of the gods. There's nothing I can't handle."

"Oh, I can think of a few things you couldn't

handle," Athena replied. "Charybdis, for instance."

"And the Minotaur!" Ares added helpfully. "Don't forget the Minotaur!"

"And the Hydra," Hermes offered.

"I get it!" Zeus cried.

"The point is," Athena continued, "we're really at our best when we're together."

"I know—we all know—we got mojo," Zeus admitted. "But you all got to go on the last adventure without me. And I've been cooped up too long." He waved at Mount Olympus. "I need to stretch my legs!"

Athena looked at Demeter for help, but the grasshopper shrugged.

"Can we at least agree to rendezvous?" Athena asked. "Say, at midnight?"

"Sure, midnight," Zeus said impatiently. He grabbed the string that ran from the boat to the top of the ramp and tossed it to Ares, who caught it with his mouth.

"Where will we meet?" Demeter asked.

"On Crete," Athena said. "Let's meet on Crete."

"Crete, sure, you bet," Zeus said quickly. "Okay, war god, heave!"

Ares tugged the string, which went taught and began dragging the boat up the ramp toward the water's edge.

"Wait!" Hermes cried. "Hold on! You haven't named yer boat!"

"It doesn't need a name," Zeus said. Ares continued pulling the string, inching Zeus and Demeter closer to the water.

"Do boat names bring good luck, too?" Demeter asked.

"Yep!" Hermes replied.

"Fine." Zeus sighed. "How about we call it …" He scratched his chin. "… the *Argo 2!*"

Athena wrinkled her nose. "I don't know about that. Sounds awfully … grandiose."

The boat was halfway up the ramp. "Fine, whatever!" Zeus snapped. "How about the *Argo ½*? That name float your boat?"

"That works," Athena said with a satisfied smile. She watched the *Argo ½* tip over the top of the ramp and— *SPLISH!*—splash into the water. It teetered but quickly settled on the calm surface of the Aegean.

Acknowledgments

Writing an adventure series is an adventure itself—complete with a cast of indispensable allies. Becky Baines at National Geographic Kids dreamed up the idea of Mount Olympus Pet Center and invited me to embark on this quest. Catherine Frank—oracle of children's literature—always finds the most exciting narrative paths for us to explore. Nat Geo's Avery Naughton keeps us from losing our way.

Illustrator Andy Elkerton continues to bring our Olympian heroes (and their spooky foes) to vivid life, while design director Amanda Larsen creates the cool look for each book. Production editor Molly Reid makes sure the world of Mount Olympus Pet Center is portrayed consistently from the first page to the last. Photo director Lori Epstein lends her expert eye.

Dr. Diane Harris Cline, a professor of history and classics at George Washington University, is my beacon for staying within sight of the source material. She's written the book on ancient Greece. Literally. It's called *The Greeks: An Illustrated History* and was as valuable to me in this process as any of Zeus's relics.

Finally, my wife, Ramah, is an endless source of inspiration and patience. She's also the wisest person I know when it comes to animals (we live on a farm). Our brave chicken Odo was the inspiration for Hermes the hen. No doubt more of our critters will find their way into future mythological escapades.

—*Crispin Boyer*

All illustrations by Andy Elkerton/Shannon Associates LLC; 196, Pamela Loreto Perez/Shutterstock; 197 (UP), kanvag/Shutterstock; 197 (LO), Rogers Fund, 1906/Metropolitan Museum of Art; 198 (UP LE), DeAgostini/Getty Images; 198 (UP CTR), Luisa Ricciarini/Leemage/Universal Images Group/Getty Images; 198 (UP RT), Gift of George Blumenthal, 1941/Metropolitan Museum of Art; 198 (LO LE), Harris Brisbane Dick Fund, 1950/Metropolitan Museum of Art; 198 (LO RT), Prisma Archivo/Alamy Stock Photo; 199 (UP LE), Adam Eastland/Alamy Stock Photo; 199 (UP CTR), The Cesnola Collection, Purchased by subscription, 1874-76/Metropolitan Museum of Art; 199 (UP RT), Fletcher Fund, 1925/Metropolitan Museum of Art; 199 (LO LE), Gift of Mrs. Frederick F. Thompson, 1903/Metropolitan Museum of Art; 199 (LO RT), Fletcher Fund, 1967/Metropolitan Museum of Art; 200 (BACKGROUND), Andrey Kuzmin/Shutterstock; 200, National Gallery of Victoria, Melbourne/Bridgeman Images